"If I asked you to dinner, would you say yes?"

Karin hadn't felt a clutch of excitement like this in years. She made a point of not dating men who were as steeped in the violent underside of human nature as she was. But standing here with Bruce in front of her, she had the oddest flash of revelation. How had she expected to fall in love with someone she couldn't talk to?

She must have been quiet for too long, because Bruce continued, "If my asking makes you uncomfortable, say so. We'll consider the subject closed."

"Yes," she said. "I mean, no. I mean…"

He stopped and faced her. Around them, the garage was brightly lit and yet somehow shadowy. They were very much alone.

"Yes? Or no?"

"Yes," she whispered. "I'd say yes."

There was that look in his eyes again, the one that seemed to liquefy her…

Dear Reader,

I have a tendency to be critical of my own writing. I'm not one of those authors who weeps with her characters, can hardly bear to let them go at the end of the book, and so on. I'm usually sure the book is lousy until I do the last read-through and am pleasantly surprised to find that it really works after all. (You'd think I would learn, wouldn't you?)

But I fell in love with Detective Bruce Walker early in the writing. Once in a while, one of my own heroes comes to life in a way I can't quite take credit for. He believes that inside him is a well of violence he never dares tap; he structures his life so that he won't end up like his abusive father. Although he proves day in and day out on the job that he's compassionate, courageous and kind, he never quite believes it. At its heart, this book is about one man, and what happens when he meets the woman who forces him to confront his ghosts and look squarely at himself. I hope you'll find his journey as wrenching as I did, and that you, too, will love a tormented, sexy hero who battles to be a decent man.

Sincerely,

Janice Kay Johnson

THE MAN
BEHIND THE COP
Janice Kay Johnson

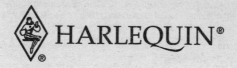

HARLEQUIN®

TORONTO • NEW YORK • LONDON
AMSTERDAM • PARIS • SYDNEY • HAMBURG
STOCKHOLM • ATHENS • TOKYO • MILAN • MADRID
PRAGUE • WARSAW • BUDAPEST • AUCKLAND

ISBN-13: 978-0-373-71489-6
ISBN-10:   0-373-71489-0

THE MAN BEHIND THE COP

Copyright © 2008 by Janice Kay Johnson.

ABOUT THE AUTHOR

Janice Kay Johnson is the author of sixty books for adults and children. She has been a finalist for a Romance Writers of America RITA® Award four times for her Harlequin Superromance novels. A former librarian, she's also worked at a juvenile court with kids involved in the foster care system. She lives north of Seattle, Washington, and is an active volunteer and board member of Purrfect Pals, a no-kill cat shelter.

Books by Janice Kay Johnson

HARLEQUIN SUPERROMANCE

HARLEQUIN SINGLE TITLE

HARLEQUIN ANTHOLOGY

SIGNATURE SELECT SAGA

HARLEQUIN EVERLASTING LOVE

†Three Good Cops
††Under One Roof
**Lost...But Not Forgotten

CHAPTER ONE

"I'M GOING TO LEAVE HIM." Determination was stark on Lenora Escobar's face, but her hands, clenched on the arms of the chair, betrayed her anxiety.

Karin Jorgensen felt a thrill of pleasure, not so much at the statement but at how far this terrorized woman had come to be able to make it. Yet Karin's alarm bells also rang, because the days and weeks after leaving an abusive man were the most dangerous time for any woman.

The two sat facing each other in Karin's office, a comfortable, cluttered space designed to allow children to play and women to feel at home. For almost five years now, Karin had been in practice with a group of psychologists at a clinic called A Woman's Hand, which offered mental health services only to women and children.

She remembered having a vague intention to go into family counseling. By good fortune, an internship here at A Woman's Hand had presented itself while she was in grad school, and she'd never looked back. Women like Lenora were her reward.

Lately, she'd begun to worry that she went way beyond

feeling mere job satisfaction when her clients took charge of their lives. She'd begun to fear they *were* her life. Their triumphs were her triumphs, their defeats her defeats. Because face it—her life outside the clinic was…bland.

Annoyed by the self-analysis, she pulled herself back to the present. *Focus,* she ordered herself. Lenora needed her.

"Are you sure you're ready for this step?" she asked.

Lenora's thin face crumpled with a thousand doubts. "Don't you think I am?"

Karin smiled gently. "I didn't say that. I'm just asking whether *you're* confident you're ready."

Two years almost to the day had passed since Lenora Escobar had come for her first appointment. In her early thirties and raising two young children, she had virtually no self-esteem. Virtually no *self.* She had come, she'd said, because her husband was so unhappy with her. She needed to change.

She'd made only three or four appointments before she disappeared for six months. When she returned, her arm was in a sling and her face was discolored with fading bruises. Even then she made excuses for him. Of course it was wrong for him to hurt her, but… She should have known better than to say this, do that. To wear a dress he didn't like. To let the kids make so much noise when he was tired after work. Only recently had she declared, "I don't want to be afraid anymore. I don't think he'll change."

In Karin's opinion, Roberto Escobar was a class-three abuser, a man as incapable of empathizing with another human being as he was of real love or remorse. Rehabilitation for this kind of offender was impossible. His need to control his wife and children would only escalate; his violence would become more extreme. If she didn't leave him, the odds were very good that eventually he would kill Lenora or one of the children.

Not that leaving him brought her any certainty that she would be safe. He had told her from their wedding night on that he *would* kill her if she ever tried to leave him. Lenora had once confessed she was flattered when he'd first said that. "He was so passionate. He told me I was his whole world."

Now she said, "I know I have to go. I guess I'm scared. I'll have to find a job, even though I've never worked. He'll be so angry…" She shivered. "But I have put a plan in place, like you advised." She talked about the safe house where staff already expected her, about the possessions she'd been sneaking out over the course of several weeks in case she had to go suddenly.

"That took courage," Karin said with approval.

"I was so afraid he'd notice when I had something tucked under my shirt or my purse was bulging! But he never did."

"How did you feel about keeping that kind of secret from him?"

"The truth?" Her face relaxed. "I felt good. Like a kid with a secret from her sister. You know?"

Karin laughed. "I do. Powerful."

"Right! Powerful." Lenora seemed to savor the word.

When had she ever been able to think of herself as powerful? "I've been looking at him and counting off the days. Thursday is payday and he always gives me money for groceries. I've been stowing some away, but a couple hundred more would be nice. So I'm going to leave Friday."

Karin nodded. "Enough for a month's rent would be great."

"But I feel I should tell him I'm going, not just disappear. After fifteen years of marriage, I think it's the least I owe him. If I had somebody there with me…"

Karin straightened in her chair. "You know how dangerous confronting him could be."

Lenora bit her lip. "Yes."

"Why do you feel you 'owe' Roberto?"

Lenora floundered, claiming at first that *owe* probably wasn't the best choice of word.

"Since I've never worked, he has brought home all the money."

"You've talked about how you would have liked to work."

She nodded. "If I'd had a paycheck of my own…"

Karin finished for her. "You would have felt more independent."

Lenora gave a small, painful smile. "He didn't want me to be independent."

Karin waited.

"You don't think I should tell him face-to-face?"

Usually, Karin let clients work their way to their own conclusion, but in this instance she said, "No. I don't think Roberto will let you walk out the door. If you have someone with you, that person will be in danger, as well. And where will the children be? What if he grabs Anna and Enrico and threatens to hurt them?"

Just audibly, Lenora confessed, "I would do anything he asked me to do."

Karin waited again.

"Okay. We'll sneak away," Lenora said.

"I really believe that's smart."

The frail woman said, "He'll come after me."

"Then you have to make sure neither you nor the children are ever vulnerable."

"I wish we could join the witness protection program or something like that."

"Just disappear," Karin said. The ultimate fantasy for a woman in Lenora's position.

Lenora nodded.

"But then you'd never see your aunt and uncle or sister again," Karin pointed out.

"They could come, too."

"Along with your sister's children? And her husband? What about *his* family?"

Lenora's eyes filled with fears and longings. "I know that can't be. But I wish."

"You realize you'll have to stay away from your family and friends for now. He'll be watching them. But if you can stay safe long enough, he'll lose interest."

Lenora agreed but didn't look convinced. And as scared as she had to be right now, who could blame her?

When the hour was over and Karin was walking her

out, Karin asked, "Will you call me once you're at the safe house?"

"Of course I will." In the reception area, furnished like a living room, Lenora hugged her. "Thank you. You've helped me more than you can imagine."

Touched, Karin hugged her back. "Thank *you.*"

Lenora drew back, sniffing. "I can keep coming here, can't I?"

"As long as you're sure he's never known about A Woman's Hand. Remember, you can't do anything predictable," Karin reminded her.

"He's never heard about this place or about you." Lenora sounded sure.

"Great. Then I'll expect you next Tuesday. Oh, and don't forget that Monday evening we're having the first class in the women's self-defense course. It would be really good for you."

They'd talked about this, too—how the course wasn't geared so much to building hand-to-hand combat skills as it was to changing the participants' confidence in themselves and teaching preparedness.

Lenora nodded. "I mentioned it to the director at the safe house, and she said she'd drive me here. She told me I could leave Enrico and Anna there, that someone would watch them, but I think I'd rather bring them. You'll have babysitting here, right?"

"Absolutely." Karin smiled and impulsively hugged her again. "Good luck."

She stood at the door and watched this amazing woman, who had defied her husband's efforts to turn her into nothing, hurry to the bus stop so she could pick up her children and be home before he was, ready to playact for three more days.

Karin seldom prayed—her faith was more bruised than her most damaged client's. But this was one of those moments when she gave wing to a silent wish.

Let her escape safely. Please let her make it.

The blue-and-white metro bus pulled to a stop, and Lenora disappeared inside it. With a sigh, Karin turned from the glass door. She had five minutes to get a cup of coffee before her next appointment, this one a fifty-eight-year-old rape survivor who'd been left for dead in the basement of her apartment building when all she'd done was go down to move her laundry from the washer to the dryer.

In the hall, Karin slowed her step briefly when she heard a woman sobbing, the sound muffled by the closed door to another office. Maybe they should have called the clinic A Woman's Tears, they ran so freely here.

Sometimes she was amazed that of the five women psychologists and counselors in practice here, three were happily married to nice men. She was grateful for the reminder that kind, patient men did exist. They might even be commonplace and not extraordinary at all. In the stories—no, the *tragedies*—that filled her days, men were the monsters, rarely the heroes.

She shook her head, discomfited by her own cynicism. This path she now walked wasn't one she'd set out on because she'd been bruised from an awful childhood or an abusive father. True, her parents had divorced, and she thought that was why she'd aimed to go into family counseling, as if the child inside her still thought she could mend her own family. But her dad was a nice man, not one of the monsters.

She couldn't deny, though, that the years here had changed her, made her look at men and women differently. She dated less and less often, as if she'd lost some capacity to hope. Which was ironic, since she spent her days trying to instill hope in other women.

In the small staff lounge, she took her mug from the cupboard.

Shaking off the inexplicable moment of malaise, she thought again, *Please let Lenora make it. Let this ending be happy.*

"MAN, I WISH *I* could shoot from the free-throw line." Grumbling, the boy snagged the ball that had just dropped, neat as you please, through the hoop.

The net itself was torn, the asphalt playground surface cracked, but playing here felt like going back to the roots of the game to Bruce Walker, who waggled his fingers. "Still my turn."

Trevor bounced the basketball hard at him. "It's not fair."

They argued mildly. The game of horse was as fair as Bruce could make it, handicapping himself so that he shot from much farther out. He pointed out that he was six feet three inches tall and had been All-Southern California in high-school basketball.

"Whereas you," he said, "are twelve years old. You've

developed a dandy layup, and you're quick. One of these days, you'll start growing an inch a week. Kid you not."

"An inch a week!" Trevor thought that was hysterical.

Bruce guessed the idea held appeal for Trevor because it transformed him into a superhero. He was at that awkward age when most boys were physically turning into young adolescents, developing muscles, growing hair. In contrast, Trevor could have been ten years old. He wasn't much over five feet tall, and so skinny even his elbows were knobby. His voice wasn't yet cracking, or even deepening. He wanted to be a man, and didn't even look like an adolescent.

Yeah, tough age.

Bruce, a homicide detective with the Seattle Police Department, had volunteered to be a Big Brother and had been paired with Trevor DeShon a year ago. He'd made the decision to offer his time as a form of payback. A cop had befriended him as a kid, making a huge difference in his life. What went around came around, Bruce figured.

Trev's mother had struggled to keep them in an apartment after Trevor's father was arrested for domestic violence. Her jaw had been wired shut for weeks after that last beating.

His dad had never hit him, Trev said, but that was because his mom always signaled him to go hide when Dad walked in the door drunk and in a bad mood. He'd huddle in his room, listening to his parents scream at each other, and would later get bags of frozen peas or corn to put on his mom's latest shiner.

Bruce didn't want Trevor growing up to be just like his dad, or turning to drugs like his mom. Maybe Bruce, by being a role model, showing Trevor there was a different kind of life out there than what he saw at home and in his rough neighborhood, could change what would otherwise be an inevitable outcome.

What Bruce hadn't expected was to worry about the kid as much as he did.

After the game of horse, they practiced layups and worked on Trevor's defensive moves, after which Bruce let him pick where to go for dinner.

That always meant pizza. Their deal was they both had a salad first so they got their vegetables. Bruce pretended not to notice how much cheese the boy put on his.

They did their best talking while they ate. Tonight, Bruce asked casually, "You heard from your dad lately?"

Trev shrugged. "He called Saturday. Mom wasn't home."

Mom would have hung up on him, Bruce knew. Trevor hadn't seen his father in two years, although the guy had tried to maintain contact, Bruce had to give him that.

"You talked to him?"

"He asked about school 'n stuff. Like you do."

"You tell him about that A in social studies?"

Trevor nodded but also hunched his shoulders. He stabbed at his lettuce with the fork and exclaimed, "Mom and me don't need *him*. I don't know why he keeps calling."

"He's your dad."

Ironic words from him, since he hadn't spoken to his

own father in years and had no intention of ever doing so again. But Trevor didn't share Bruce's feelings toward his father. The boy tried to hide how glad he was that his dad hadn't given up, but it shone on his face sometimes.

"I wish you were," Trevor mumbled.

Bruce felt a jolt of alarm. He'd been careful never to pretend he was a substitute father. He didn't have it in him to be a father of any kind, even a pretend one.

"If you were my dad," Trevor continued, "I could tell everyone my dad has a badge and a gun and they better watch out if they disrespect me."

Thank God. The kid didn't want Bruce as a father; he wanted him for show-and-tell.

Diagnosing the true problem, Bruce asked, "You still having trouble with that guy at the bus stop?"

"Sometimes," the twelve-year-old admitted. "Mostly, I walk real slow so I don't get there until the bus is coming. 'Cuz if the driver sees anything, Jackson gets detention."

Bruce had tried to figure out what he could do to help, but he couldn't walk a middle schooler to the bus stop and threaten a thirteen-year-old kid. A couple of times, he had picked Trevor up at school, making sure to drive his unmarked vehicle, which even an unsophisticated middle schooler would still spot as a squad car. Mostly, his goal was to help Trevor gain the confidence to handle a little shit like Jackson by himself.

He glanced at his watch and said, "I've got to get you home. I'm teaching a self-defense class tonight."

Scrambling out of the booth, Trevor chopped the air. "Like karate and stuff? Wow! I bet you have a black belt."

Bruce appreciated the boy's faith, but he laughed. "No, in my neighborhood how we fought didn't have a fancy name. Anyway, this class is for women. I teach them how to walk down a street and not look like a victim. How to break a hold if someone grabs them." How to fight dirty if things got down to it, but he didn't tell Trevor that. He wasn't going to teach him how to put out an assailant's eye. Jackson might be a bully, but he didn't deserve to be blinded.

Bruce was volunteering his time to teach this class for the same reason he'd signed up to be a Big Brother: his own screwed-up family. If he could help one woman choose not to be a victim the way his own mother was, he didn't begrudge sparing any amount of time. He couldn't change who he was, and he'd long since given up on trying to rescue his mother. But he was bleeding heart enough to still think he could rescue other people.

Trevor lived in White Center, a neighborhood on the south end of Seattle known for high crime and drug use. Bruce had guessed from the beginning that MaryBeth DeShon, the boy's mother, was using. At twenty-eight, she was pathetically young to have a kid Trevor's age. She hadn't finished high school and lacked job skills. Since Bruce had known them, MaryBeth had worked as a waitress, but she was constantly changing jobs. Not by choice, Trevor had admitted. She didn't feel good sometimes, he said, and had to miss work. Bosses weren't understanding. Still, she'd managed to bring in something approaching a living wage, and had food stamps, as well.

Often Bruce didn't see her when he picked up and dropped off Trevor. The last time he had, two weeks ago, she'd looked so bad he'd been shocked. She'd always been thin, but now she was so skinny, pasty and jittery he'd immediately thought, *Crack*. He'd been worrying ever since.

"Your mom—how is she?" he asked now, a few blocks from Trevor's apartment building.

The boy's shoulders jerked. "She's gone a lot. You know?" Trev was trying hard not to sound worried, but his anxiety bled into his voice. His instincts were good. He might not know why he was losing his mother, but he was smart enough to be scared. "She says she's looking for work. Sometimes Mrs. Porter checks on me."

Sometimes? Bruce's hands tightened on the steering wheel. A kid Trevor's age shouldn't habitually be home alone at night, especially not in this neighborhood. But he was twelve, and leaving him without adult supervision wasn't a crime.

Bruce pulled into the apartment parking lot, and noticed that MaryBeth's slot was empty. "Doesn't look like she's home right now," he observed. Although it seemed possible to him that her piece-of-crap car had finally gone to the great wrecking yard in the sky.

Trevor shrugged and reached for the door handle. "I have a key."

"If you get scared, you call me, okay?"

"Yeah. Thanks. I'm okay, though."

Bruce reached out and ruffled Trevor's brown hair.

"You're a great kid. But you are a kid. So call me if you need me."

He was usually in a good mood after a day spent with Trevor, but this time his eyebrows drew together as he walked back to his car after leaving Trevor at the door and waiting to hear the lock click home.

I should have asked if the kitchen was decently stocked, he thought repentantly. MaryBeth sure as hell wasn't eating these days. If she was hardly ever home, would she remember to grocery-shop? Assuming she hadn't traded her food stamps for crack.

He'd call tomorrow, Bruce decided. Check to see if she'd reappeared, satisfy himself that Trev was okay. Frustrating as it was for him, a man used to taking charge, there wasn't much else he could do for the boy.

It bothered him how much he wished there was.

BRUCE HAD PREVIOUSLY driven by A Woman's Hand, the mental health clinic where he was to conduct the self-defense workshop that night. It was in a modern but plain brick building off Madison, the simple sign out front not indicative of the services offered within. He supposed that was because of the clientele, the majority of whom were victims of abuse. A woman cop in the sexual assault unit told him she referred every victim she encountered to A Woman's Hand.

"The counselors there are the best," she'd said simply.

When he arrived, it was already dark, but the building and parking lot were well lit. The small lot was full. Amid all the cars, he noticed the two plain vans, which he guessed were from battered women's shelters. He had to drive a couple of blocks before he found a spot on a residential street to park his car.

When he got back to the clinic, he found the front door locked. Smart. He knocked, and through the glass he saw a woman hurrying to open the door. He allowed himself a brief moment of appreciation. Tall and long-legged, she had a fluid walk that was both athletic and unmistakably feminine. Hair the rich gold of drying cornstalks was bundled up carelessly, escaping strands softening the businesslike effect.

Her expression was suspicious when she unlocked and pushed the door open a scant foot. He took a mental snapshot: great cheekbones, sensual mouth, bump on the bridge of her nose. Around thirty, he guessed. No wedding ring, a surreptitious glance determined.

"May I help you?" she asked.

"I'm Detective Bruce Walker," he said, unclipping his shield from his belt and holding it out for her to see. "I was invited to lead this self-defense workshop."

A tentative smile warmed her face, but she also peered past him in apparent puzzlement. "Welcome. But weren't you to have a partner?"

"Detective Beckstead will be joining us next week. She's the labor coach for her pregnant sister, whose water broke this afternoon."

He'd been hearing about the birthing classes from Molly Beckstead for the past two months. She was unmarried, hadn't yet contemplated having a baby herself, and when she was a rookie had been scarred for life, she claimed, by having to assist a woman giving birth in the back seat of a taxicab. All spring, she'd provided weekly reports on the horrors of childbirth, half tongue-in-cheek, half serious, but he'd noticed she sounded more excited than terrified when she'd called to tell him she was meeting her sister at the hospital.

"Ah." The woman relaxed. "That's an excuse if I've ever heard one." She pushed the door farther open to allow him in. "I'm sorry to seem less than welcoming. Some of the women participating tonight are from battered women's shelters, and we always keep in mind the possibility that the men in their lives might be following them."

"I understand. And you are…?"

"Karin Jorgensen. I'm a counselor here at A Woman's Hand."

"You're the one who set this up. Good to meet you." He held out his hand, and they shook. He liked her grip, firm and confident, and the feel of her fine-boned hand in his. In fact, he let go of it reluctantly.

"This way," she said, leading him down the hall. "The women are all here. I hope our space is big enough for the purpose. It's the first time we've done anything like this, and if this venue doesn't work well tonight, we could plan to use a weight room or gym at a school the next time. We're just more comfortable with the security here."

He nodded. "I'm sure it will be fine. For the most part, we won't be doing many throws. With only the four sessions, we can't turn the women into martial artists.

We'll focus more on attitude and on how they can talk their way out of situations."

She stopped at a door, from behind which he heard voices. She lowered her own. "You are aware that most of these women have already been beaten or raped?"

He held her gaze, surprised that her eyes were brown, although her hair was blond. Was it blond from a bottle? His lightning-quick evaluation concluded no. She was the unusual natural blonde who had warm, chocolate-brown eyes.

"I'll be careful not to say anything to make the women feel they've failed in any way."

The smile he got was soft and beautiful. "Thank you." The next moment, she opened the door and gestured for him to precede her into the room.

Heads turned, and Bruce found himself being inspected. Not every woman appeared alarmed, but enough did that Bruce wondered if they'd expected only a woman cop. Ages ranged from late teens to mid fifties or older, their clothing style, from street kid to moneyed chic. But what these women had in common mattered more than their differences.

He was careful to move slowly, to keep his expression pleasant.

Karin Jorgensen introduced him, then stepped back and stood in a near-parade stance, as though to say *I'm watching you.*

Good. He had his eye on her, too.

Bruce smiled and looked from face to face. "My partner, Molly, asked me to apologize for her. Her sister is in labor, and Molly is her labor coach. She plans to be here next week. Tonight, you get just me."

He saw some tense shoulders and facial muscles relax, as if the mention of a woman giving birth and another there to hold her hand somehow reassured them. The support of other women was all that was helping some of his audience, he guessed.

"We'll work on a few self-defense drills toward the end of the session—I don't want you to get numb sitting and listening to me talk," he began. "But we'll focus more on physical self-defense in coming weeks. It'll be easier for me to demonstrate with my partner's help. She's just five feet five inches tall, but she can take me down." He paused to let them absorb that. He was six foot three and solidly built. If a woman ten inches shorter than him could protect herself against him, even be the aggressor, they were definitely interested.

"Most women I know have been raised to believe the men in their lives will protect them," he continued. "That's a man's role. A woman's is to let herself be protected. How can women be expected to defend themselves against men? You're smaller, lighter, finer boned, carry less muscle and are incapable of aggression." He looked around the circle of perhaps twenty women sitting in chairs pushed against the walls of what he guessed was a large conference room. When the silence had stretched long enough, Bruce noted, "That's the stereotype. Here's reality. Throughout nature, mother animals are invariably the fiercest of their kind. Like men, women want to survive. Nature creates all of us with that instinct. You, too, can fight if you have to."

The quiet was absolute. They were hanging on his every word. They wanted to believe him, with a hunger he understood only by context.

"Do you have disadvantages if you're attacked by a guy my size?" He ambled around the room, focusing on one woman at a time, doing his best to maintain an un-threatening posture. "Sure. What I'm here to tell you is that you have advantages, too. You're likely quicker than I am, for one thing. You've got a lower center of gravity. Women are famous for their intuition, for their ability to read mood and intentions. Chances are good you can outthink your attacker. And if you're prepared, you're going to shock him. He won't expect you to fight back. He'll have the surprise of his life."

Murmurs, surprise of their own, but also a gathering sense of possibility: *Maybe he's right. Maybe I can outwit and outfight a man.*

He told them stories of women who'd had an assailant whimpering on the ground by the time they were done.

"The greatest battle you have to fight from here on out," he went on, "is with your own attitude. What you have to do is liberate yourself from every defeatist voice you've ever heard.

"Many of you have already been assaulted." Heads bobbed, and renewed fear seemed to shiver from woman to woman, as if a whisper had made the rounds. "Then I don't have to tell you submission doesn't work." He waited for more nods, these resigned. "I'm here to tell you aggression might. At worst—" he spread his hands "—you'll be injured. But you know what? He was going to hurt you anyway."

Something was coming alive in their faces. They looked at one another, exchanged more nods.

He had them, from the frail Hispanic woman in the corner, to the overweight teenage girl with acne, to the iron-haired woman who could have been his mother had Mom ever had the courage to seek the means to defend herself.

And, he saw, he had pleased Karin Jorgensen, who at last abandoned her military stance by the door and took a seat, prepared to listen and learn, herself.

He didn't let her sit for long, asking her to help him demonstrate. As he showed how an attacker opened himself up the minute he reached out to fumble with clothing or lift a hand to strike, Bruce was pleased by tiny signs that Karin was as aware of him physically as he was of her. Nothing that would catch anyone else's attention—just a quiver of her hand, a touch of warmth in her cheeks, a shyness in her gaze—all were a contrast to the confident woman who'd opened the door to him, prepared to face him down if he'd been anyone but the cop she expected.

She smelled good, he noticed when he grabbed her, although the scent was subtle. Tangy, like lemon. Maybe just a shampoo. Lemon seemed right for her sun-streaked hair.

He wanted to keep her with him, but finally thanked

her and said, "Okay, everyone pair up." Unfortunately, the numbers were odd and she paired herself with an overweight teenager, which left him partnerless.

A fair amount of the next hour and a half was spent with him trying to prepare them to grab their first opportunity to fight back and run. They learned some simple techniques for breaking holds or knocking a weapon from an assailant's hand.

"Next week," he said, concluding, "we'll talk about how to use everyday objects as weapons and shields. Molly will be here to demonstrate more releases, more ways to drop me like a rock." He smiled. "See you then."

Several women came up afterward to talk to him. By the time Bruce looked around for Karin, she had disappeared. When he went out into the hall to find her, he realized that some of the women had brought children. A second room had evidently been dedicated to child care. He spotted her in there, holding a toddler and talking to one of the participants. Karin saw him at the same time, and handed the toddler to the mother, then walked over to him.

"I'll escort you out," she said. "I appreciate you doing this."

They started down the hall, her long-legged stride matching his. "I thought it went well," Bruce commented.

"It was amazing. I saw such…hope." She said the word oddly, with some puzzlement.

Had he surprised her? Given her job, maybe she didn't like men much and didn't think one was capable of inspiring a group of battered women.

Or maybe she'd just been groping for the right word.

He wanted to ask whether she was married or involved, but how could he without making things awkward? And, damn it, he was running out of time— the front door stood just ahead.

"I understand you volunteered for this workshop," Karin said. "That's very generous of you."

They'd reached the door. Opening it for her, he inquired, "Are you making any money for this evening's work?"

He'd surprised her again. She paused, close enough for him to catch another whiff of citrus scent. For a moment she searched his face, as if trying to understand him. "Well…no. But I do work with these women."

"I do, too," he said simply.

She bit her lip. "Oh."

"'Night, Karin," someone called, and she retreated from him, going outside to exchange good-nights with women on their way to their cars.

Maybe just as well, he tried to convince himself as he, too, exited the building. He'd ask around about her. They inhabited a small world, and someone would know whether she was off limits. If nothing else, he'd see her next week.

"Good night," he said, nodding. He'd finally snagged her attention.

"Thank you again," she replied.

Their eyes met and held for a moment that seemed to bring color to her cheeks. Wishful thinking, maybe. He turned away. Even with his back to Karin, he was aware of her speaking to others in the parking lot. The voices, he was glad to hear, were animated.

He kept going, enjoying the cool air and the way the scent of the lilacs was sharper after dark. He liked the night and the sense he had of being invisible. He could see people moving around inside their houses or the flicker of televisions through front windows, but by now not a single car passed him on the street.

He reached his car, now sandwiched between an SUV and a VW Beetle. Not much room to maneuver. He'd be inching out.

His key was in his hand, but he hadn't yet inserted it in the door, when he heard the first terrified scream.

CHAPTER TWO

IT HAPPENED SO FAST.

The parking lot had emptied quickly. Only a van from one of the battered women's shelters remained, the director half sitting on the bumper as she awaited her charge. Satisfied with how the evening had gone, Karin was walking back toward the front door of the clinic when, out of the corner of her eye, she caught movement under a streetlight. She turned to see a dark figure rush toward the lone woman halfway between the building and the van. Oh, God. It was Lenora Escobar. She'd just said good-night to Karin.

"Roberto!"

The distinctly uttered name struck terror in Karin.

His arm lifted. He held a weapon of some kind. Lenora screamed.

The weapon smashed down followed by an indescribably horrible sound. Like a pumpkin being dropped, squishing. Lenora gurgled, then crumpled.

The arm rose and fell a second time, and then Roberto Escobar ran.

During the whole event, Karin hadn't managed two steps forward.

As though time became real once more, Karin and Cecilia, the shelter director, converged on the fallen woman. Karin focused only on her, ignoring the squealing tires from the street.

Should I have run after him? Tried to make out a license-plate number?

But no. There could be no doubt that Lenora's assailant—not her murderer, please not her murderer—was her husband. His vehicle and license-plate number would be on record.

Thank God, Karin thought, dropping to her knees, that Lenora hadn't brought her children tonight. He would have taken them if she had.

Lenora's head lay in a pool of blood. A few feet away was a tire iron. Karin's stomach lurched. Fingerprints... Had Roberto worn gloves? No. He didn't care who knew that he'd killed his wife for the sin of leaving him.

"Cecilia, go back inside and call 911. Or do you have a cell phone?" She sounded almost calm. "Unless... wait." She heard pounding footsteps and swiveled on her heels. "Detective Walker," she said with profound relief—relief she felt not just because he was a cop and he was *here,* but because tonight this particular cop had managed to reassure and inspire a roomful of women who had every reason to be afraid of men.

He was running across the parking lot, holding a cell phone in his hand. Then he was crouching beside her. He spoke urgently into the phone, giving numbers she guessed were code for Battered Wife Down.

He touched Lenora's neck and looked up. "She's alive."

Karin sagged. "Can't we do anything?"

He shook his head. "We don't want to move her. The ambulance is on its way." His gaze, razor sharp, rested on Karin's face. "Did you see what happened?"

"Yes." To Karin's embarrassment, her voice squeaked. So much for calm. She cleared her throat. "It was her husband. She said the name Roberto. She just left him."

"She and her children are staying at the shelter," Cecilia added. "She didn't tell him she was leaving him. I don't know how he found her."

"He had to have followed her tonight." The detective was thinking aloud. "Where are the children? He didn't get them?"

Cecilia was a dumpy, endlessly comforting woman likely in her fifties. Detective Walker hadn't even finished his question before she shook her head. "Lenora's aunt picked them up and took them home for the night. She's to bring them back in the morning."

Karin's heart chilled at his expression. "You don't think…?" Oh, God. If he had the aunt's house staked out…

She'd warned Lenora. "Stay away from friends and family," she'd said.

Focused on Cecilia, Detective Walker asked, "Do you know the woman's name?"

"Yes…um, Lopez. Señora Lopez."

Aunt:… Karin groped in her memory. Aunt… "Julia."

"Yes." Cecilia flashed her a grateful look. "Julia Lopez. I have her phone number back at the shelter."

"Call." He held out his cell phone. "We need to send a unit over there. She should know about her niece, anyway."

"Yes. Of course." Cecilia fumbled with the phone but finally dialed.

Karin didn't listen. She stared helplessly at Lenora, who had been so triumphant Friday afternoon because she'd successfully made her getaway. "He never guessed anything," she'd told Karin in amazement. "He gave me money Thursday after he deposited his check. He was even in a good mood."

Now, gazing at Lenora's slack face and blood-matted hair, Karin could only say, "He followed her aunt to the shelter tonight, didn't he?"

At the first wail of a siren, Karin's head came up. She prayed fervently, *Let it be the ambulance for Lenora.*

A second siren played a chorus. Two vehicles arrived in a rush. A Seattle PD car first, flying into the parking lot, then the ambulance, coming from the opposite direction.

The EMTs took over. As Karin stood and backed away to give them room to work, her legs trembled as though she'd run a marathon. And not just her legs. She was shaking all over, she realized. For all the stories she'd heard from brutalized women, she'd never witnessed a rape scene or murder or beating. The experience was quite different in real life.

Cecilia came to her and they hugged, then clung. Karin realized her face was wet with tears.

Bruce Walker was busy issuing orders to two uniformed officers. Their voices were low and urgent; beyond them, in the squad car, the radio crackled.

"We should wait inside," Karin said at last. She needed to sit. "He'll probably want to ask us both some more questions."

Cecilia drew a shuddering breath. "Yes. You're right."

Karin glanced back, to find that Detective Walker was watching them. He gave her a nod, which she interpreted as approval. His air of command was enormously comforting.

Thank God he'd still been within earshot. Imagine how much harder this would be had she been dealing with strangers now, instead.

The gurney vanished into the guts of the aid car, one of the EMTs with it. The other EMT slammed the back doors and raced to the driver's side of the vehicle. They were moving so fast, not wasting a motion. Then once again the siren wailed, and the ambulance roared down the street.

She couldn't stop herself from looking again at the blood slick, dark under the streetlight, and at the tire iron, flung like some obscene kind of cross on the pavement. Then the two women walked into the building, still holding hands.

HE CAME IN sooner than she expected, thank goodness.

Through the glass doors, both women were aware of the blinding white flashes as a photographer worked, a counterpoint to the blue-and-white lights from the squad car. *Why don't they turn them off?* Karin wondered, anger sparking. What *good* did they do?

Once inside, the detective walked straight to them and sank into a chair beside Karin. Turning his body so that he was facing them, he was so close to Karin his knee bumped hers and she could see the bristles on his jaw. Like most dark-haired men, he must need to shave twice a day to keep a smooth jaw. But then, this day had been longer than he could ever have anticipated.

Karin gave her head a shake. Did it matter how well groomed he was? No. Yet she couldn't seem to discipline her thoughts. She *wanted* to think about something, anything, but that awful smash-squish and the sight of Lenora collapsing. Karin had never seen anyone fall like that, with no attempt to regain footing or fling out arms to break the impact. As if Lenora had already been dead, and it didn't matter how she hit.

Detective Walker pulled a small notebook and pen from a pocket inside his leather jacket. With a few succinct questions, he extracted a bald description of events from Cecilia, then Karin.

"Thank the Lord the other women had gone," Cecilia said with a sigh.

"Amen," Karin breathed. Imagine if Olivia, recently raped and still emotionally fragile, had witnessed the brutal assault.

The shelter director asked, "Have you heard anything about the aunt?"

"Not yet."

Was he worried? Karin scrutinized his face. She couldn't be sure—she didn't know him—but thought she saw tiny signs of tension beside his eyes, in muscles bunched in his jaw, in the way he reached up and squeezed his neck, grimacing.

"This was a bad idea," Karin exclaimed. "To bring all these women here like…like sitting ducks! What was I thinking?"

He laid his hand over hers. "No, it was a good idea," he reassured her quietly, those intense eyes refusing to let her look away from him. "Once Roberto knew where his wife was, it was a done deal."

"It's true," Cecilia assured her. "Don't you remember? Just last year, Janine's boyfriend was waiting outside the shelter for her. He shot her, then himself, right there on the sidewalk. It was—" She stopped, sinking her teeth into her lip. "This could just as easily have happened at the shelter. Lenora had to go out eventually."

Karin deliberately relaxed her hands, and he removed his. What was she doing, thinking about herself now? Her guilt could wait. Right now the children mattered; Lenora mattered. Karin was wasting this man's time making him console her, when he should be doing something to catch Roberto.

"Do you know which hospital they took Lenora to?" she asked.

"Harborview. It's tops for trauma." His cell phone rang. "Excuse me."

He stood and walked away, but not outside. Although his back was to them, Karin heard his sharp expletive. Her hand groped Cecilia's.

Still talking, he faced them. His eyes sought out Karin's, and she saw anger in them. It chilled her, and she gripped the director's hand more tightly. He listened, talked and listened some more, never looking away from her.

Finally he ended the call and came back to them. Karin wasn't sure she'd even blinked. She couldn't tear her gaze from this man's.

He dropped into the chair as if exhausted. "He's already been there. The aunt's dead. A neighbor says the uncle works a night shift. We'll be tracking him down next. The kids are gone."

"Oh, no," Karin breathed, although his expression had told her what happened before he'd said a word. Cecilia exclaimed, too.

"I'm heading over there. I'm Homicide. This case—" his voice hardened "—I'm taking personally."

"The children…" Horror seized Karin by the throat. "Does that mean they were in the car? Did they *see* him attack their mother?"

Detective Walker's mouth twisted. "We don't know yet. He had a headstart. He could have gotten there, killed the aunt and snatched the kids after leaving here."

She heard the doubt in his voice. "But…?"

"The officers who found her haven't found a weapon. She was battered in the head. She could be lying on it, or it might be tossed under a bush in the front yard."

Something very close to a sob escaped Karin. "But he might have used the same tire iron."

"Possibly."

"I pray they didn't see," Cecilia whispered. "Enrico and Anna are the nicest, best-behaved children. Their faces shone for their mother."

"Have…have you heard anything?" Karin asked. "About Lenora?"

"Nothing." His hand lifted, as if he intended to touch her again, and then his fingers curled into a fist and he stood. Expression heavy with pity, he said, "There's no need for you to stay."

"I'm going to the hospital." Karin rose to her feet, too, galvanized now by purpose, however little hovering in a hospital waiting room really served. *She* couldn't save Lenora, but somebody should be there, and who else was there until family was located?

Cecilia nodded, rising, as well. "I have to go back to the shelter first and talk to the residents. I don't want them to hear about this from anyone else. I asked staff to wait. I'll join you as soon as I can, Karin."

"Thank you." Karin squeezed Cecilia's hand one more time, then released it. She turned to the detective. "You'll let us know?"

He nodded. "Do you have a cell phone?"

She told him her number and watched him write it down in his small, spiral notebook. And then he inclined his head, said, "Ladies," and left.

Neither woman moved for a minute, both watching through the glass as he crossed the parking lot, spoke to officers still out there, then disappeared into the darkness.

"He's…impressive," Cecilia said at last.

"Yes." Thank goodness Cecilia had no way of knowing how attracted she'd been to him from the moment she'd let him into the clinic. Embarrassed, she cleared her throat. "I hope…" She didn't finish the thought.

Didn't have to. Cecilia nodded and sighed. "What's to become of those poor children?"

"Lenora has a sister in this country. She has children, too. I'm not sure whether they're in the Seattle area." Once they talked to Lenora's uncle, he'd make calls.

Karin shut off lights and locked up. Activity in the parking lot had slowed and the tire iron had apparently been bagged and removed, but a uniformed officer asked that they exit carefully, pulling out so as not to drive over the crime scene. Somebody, Karin saw, was vacuuming around the bloodstain. Trace evidence could make or break a case, she knew, but how would they be able to sift out anything meaningful from the normal debris?

Following her gaze, Cecilia murmured, "What a terrible night," and got into her van.

Karin hit the locks once she was in her car, inserted the key and started the engine, then began to shake again. She was shocked at her reaction. She'd always tended to stay levelheaded in minor emergencies, whereas other people panicked. *Minor,* she thought wryly, *was the operative word.* Bruce Walker had been angry, but utterly controlled, while here she was, falling apart.

She sat in the car for easily two minutes, until her hands were steady when she lifted them. Finally, she was able to back out, and followed the police officer's gestures to reach the street.

At a red light, she checked to make sure her cell phone was on and the battery not exhausted. How long, she wondered, until she heard from Detective Bruce Walker? And why did it seem so important that he not delegate that call?

BRUCE HADN'T TOLD the women that what he most feared was finding Anna and Enrico Escobar dead at their father's hand, next to his body.

Bruce had gone straight to the Lopez home, but on the way he made the necessary calls to get a warrant to go into the Escobar house. If the son of a bitch had intended to take his whole family out, it seemed logical that he'd have gone home with the kids. He might have feared being stopped in the parking lot before he finished the job.

God, Bruce hated domestic abuse cases. Every single one struck too close to home for him.

The woman who now lay dead just inside the front door looked disquietingly like her niece—unfortunately, down to the depressed skull and blood-soaked black hair. Unlike her niece, she had tried to defend herself, though. Her forearm was clearly broken.

Gazing down at her, he thought, *So, Dad, what would you think of this? To keep order in his own house, does a man have the right to kill not just his wife, but her relatives, too?*

Not that his own mother was dead, although she seemed more ghostlike than real to Bruce.

He had barely time for a quick evaluation of the Lopez murder scene before the warrant for a search of the Escobar house came through. Wishing Molly were with him, he snagged a uniformed officer to accompany him to the Escobars'.

They turned off headlights and coasted to a stop at the curb in front of the small place, but the minute Bruce saw that it was dark he knew they'd find it empty. The front door, he discovered after one hard knock, wasn't even locked. No, Escobar hadn't worried about protecting his possessions.

Walking through, Bruce tried to decide whether the place had an air of abandonment because Lenora had moved out with the kids, or Roberto Escobar, too, had departed with no intention of returning.

Near the telephone in the kitchen, a fist-size hole was punched in the wall. Plaster dust littered the otherwise clean countertop. Had Lenora laid the note here, by the phone, telling her husband she'd left him? One of the kitchen chairs was also smashed, and lay in the corner behind the table. Roberto had read the note, thrown a temper tantrum and sworn he'd find his wife and punish her.

It was hard to tell in the small master bedroom whether he'd packed. Lenora hadn't taken all her clothes, and some of his hung in the closet, as well. But Bruce found no coats and, more tellingly, no shaving kit or toothbrush in the bathroom. The tiny bedroom the children had apparently shared looked as though a burglar had ransacked it. Maybe Escobar had been trying to find a few toys and clothes for his kids.

Bruce poked into the single, detached garage and down in the dank, unfinished basement just in case, before finally sealing the property with tape. He'd come back tomorrow, in better light, to see what else he could learn. Right now, he was glad to have found the place deserted. That gave him hope that Escobar intended to run with the children, not murder them out of spite.

But there was no guarantee they wouldn't find the bodies in his car, parked in some alley, or... It was the "or" that stopped Bruce. He hated knowing so little. He couldn't even speculate on where Escobar might go to hide or to commit suicide.

Because he couldn't resist the temptation, Bruce called to let Karin Jorgensen know they hadn't located Escobar and to find out whether she'd gotten any word on the wife's condition.

"She's out of surgery, but in a coma. They...don't sound hopeful."

He wasn't hopeful, either. He'd seen Lenora Escobar's head, and the blood, bone splinters and other tissue on the tire iron. He wondered whether they ought to be hoping she *didn't* survive. He, for one, wouldn't want to wake up at all if it meant living in a vegetative state or anything approaching one. He wasn't sure it would be much better if she woke up clear and present to be told that her aunt had been murdered and her children taken by the violent man Lenora had fled.

"Do me a favor and think back to anything Lenora ever told you that would suggest a place Escobar might go to ground. Does he have family in this country? In Mexico? Did she talk about friends? Hell, I don't suppose they have a summer cabin."

"No, I'm pretty sure they weren't in that economic stratum. Uh..." She sounded muzzy, not surprising given that it was—Bruce glanced at his watch—3:00 a.m. Likely her adrenaline hadn't yet allowed her to curl up in the waiting room and conk out.

"She didn't talk about friends," Karin continued. "I don't think he encouraged them, at least not for her. Maybe not for him, either. He was jealous, of course. He'd imagine any other man would be coveting her, I'm afraid. As for family—his mother used to live with them, but she decided to go back to Mexico last year." Silence suggested Karin was thinking. "Chiapas. That's what Lenora said. Roberto was mad that she went."

"Chiapas." He pinched the bridge of his nose. "So I suppose it's reasonable that he might run for Mexico."

"Maybe. But how would even a mother take the news that he'd killed his wife—*tried* to kill his wife," she corrected herself, a hitch in her voice, "and murdered his wife's aunt?"

"Depends on the mother. I've met some crazy ones."

"You mean, the ones who pay a hit man to knock off the judge or prosecutor?"

"Or a rival cheerleader," he noted dryly.

"Well…yes. But I had the impression Mama had thrown up her hands over Roberto. There was another son, if I remember right, still in Chiapas. But Roberto was the elder, so of course he thought she should stay here."

"What—to babysit and keep a stern eye on his wife?" Bruce loosed a tired sigh. "No sign he's bought airline, Amtrak or bus tickets, and we've got the state patrol here and in Oregon watching for his car. Sounds like it's a beater, though. I doubt he'd make it all the way to the border, never mind damn near to Guatemala. I think you're right about the economic stratum." He paused. "How'd she pay for the sessions with you?"

"Department of Social and Health Services program. When a woman or child needs us, we find funding."

"Ah." He softened his voice. "You should get some sleep, Ms. Jorgensen."

"Karin."

"Karin. The night's not done."

"No." Her breathing told him she hadn't hung up. "I just keep thinking…"

Understanding stabbed him. "You've never been assaulted?"

"No. And now I'm thinking how—how *glib* I must have sounded to women who have. Ugh."

God. Here he'd considered her as a colleague, in a sense, who'd seen it all. Of course she hadn't. She'd only *heard* it all.

"I've been told by people who know that you and your colleagues at A Woman's Hand are the best. I doubt you've been glib."

Even through the phone line, her exhalation sounded ragged. "Thank you for that. And for calling. Oh. Have you talked to Lenora's sister yet?"

"Sorry. I meant to say that first. They're in Walla Walla. Asparagus harvest. No phone—I had to send an officer around. But they're on their way. What is it—a three-, four-hour drive? They should be at the hospital by dawn."

"Thank goodness. When Lenora wakes up…"

An optimist. He'd guessed she would be. He was

well aware that he'd be wasting his breath to suggest she go home and go to bed. She felt responsible, justly or not, and wouldn't let herself off the hook. Lenora wouldn't know Karin was holding vigil, but Karin did, and would think less of herself if she didn't.

There wasn't much more he could do tonight. He'd sent officers out to canvass near neighbors to Julia and Mateo Lopez shortly after the body was found. None had heard a thing. Evidence techs had taken over the house and were still working. He wouldn't get results from the crime lab on exactly whose blood was on the tire iron until tomorrow at best. He knew damn well what the results would be, given that no weapon had been located in or near the Lopez home.

There was a limit to how much he could do before morning to find Escobar's rat hole, either. He'd put out the description of the vehicle and the license number, but not until tomorrow would he be able to access bank records or speak to co-workers and—if any existed—friends. Mateo was so distraught he'd had to be sedated. Bruce hadn't gotten much out of him, not once he'd been told about his wife.

Resisting the temptation to drive to Harborview and keep Karin Jorgensen company in the waiting room, Bruce went home. Tomorrow would be a long day. He'd done what he could tonight to set a manhunt in motion. Now he needed a few hours of downtime.

Funny thing, how he fell asleep picturing Karin Jorgensen. Not with her face distraught, but from earlier in the evening, when she'd still been able to smile.

CHAPTER THREE

BRUCE SLEPT for four hours and awoke Tuesday morning feeling like crap. He grunted at the sight of his face in the mirror and concentrated after that on the path of the electric razor, not on the overall picture. Coffee helped enough that he realized the ring of the telephone had awakened him. He checked voice mail, and found a message from Molly.

"Houston, we have a launch. Baby Elizabeth Molly—yes, named for me—was born at 5:25 this morning. While you were no doubt sleeping, ah, like a baby."

Ha! He grinned.

"Since *I* didn't have an indolent eight hours of beauty sleep," she continued, "I'm taking Fiona and baby home and crashing—Elizabeth Molly permitting—in Fiona's guest room." As an obvious afterthought, she added, "Hope the self-defense workshop went well." Beep.

Oh, if only you knew.

He skipped breakfast, figuring to get something out of the vending machine at the hospital.

Karin had gone home, he found, and was surprised at his disappointment. Instead, the waiting room was filled with Lenora Escobar's extended family. The sister and husband and their brood of five children, and one of the Lopez's four grown children with *his* wife. Lenora, he was told, was still unresponsive in ICU.

He asked to speak privately with Lenora's sister and her husband, and took them to a smaller room likely saved by hospital officials for the grave business of telling family a loved one hadn't made it. Tending to claustrophobia, Bruce left the door open.

Yolanda spoke English well, her husband less so. They switched to Spanish, in which Bruce had become fluent on the job. He'd started with Seattle PD on a beat in a predominantly Hispanic neighborhood, building on his high-school Spanish.

Both told him that they had always thought Roberto was scum. "Pah!" Alvaro Muñoz declared. "You could see the bruises, how frightened she was of him. But she lied to make us believe everything was fine. Only recently…" A lean, mustachioed man, he hesitated, glancing at his wife.

"She told me she was going to leave him. She said so on the phone. She lowered her voice, so I think maybe he was home. She said she'd call when she got to the safe house." She bit her lip in distress. "Did he hear when she told me?"

Bruce shook his head. "Your aunt Julia went to the shelter to pick the kids up. I suspect Roberto was following her."

Yolanda Muñoz was petite like her sister, but pleasantly rounded. Her husband's skin was leathery from the sun, but hers was a soft café au lait. She must stay at home with the children, whatever home might be, given what Bruce gathered was their migrant lifestyle. Grief made her voice tremulous, kept her eyes moist. "You'll find Anna and Enrico?" she demanded. "When Lenora wakes up, how can I tell her *he* has them?"

He offered his automatic response. "We're doing our best. What I'm hoping you can do is tell me everything you know about Roberto. We'll be talking to his co-workers, but what about friends? Hobbies?" Seeing perplexity on their faces, he realized the concept of hobbies was foreign to them, as hard as they worked and as careful as they likely were with every penny they earned. "Ah…did he go fishing? Work on cars?"

Both heads shook in unison. "He didn't like to leave Lenora alone," Yolanda explained. "Even when family was there, so was he. All women in the kitchen, and Roberto. As if he thought we'd talk about him."

Or as if he couldn't let his wife have anything that was hers alone, even the easy relationship with her family.

Bruce continued to ask questions, but they knew frustratingly little. Roberto Escobar worked. Yes, he was a hard worker, they agreed, the praise grudging but fairly given, and he did help keep their place nice. He talked about his mother coming to live with them again. He was angry when she went to live with his brother, instead. Lenora said he called the mother sometimes, but mostly he yelled, so they didn't know if he would take the children to her. Yolanda thought maybe his mother liked Lenora better than her own son. And who could blame her?

Yolanda and her husband rejoined their children and cousins, and Bruce drove to the lumberyard where Escobar had worked. There, he learned little. Co-workers thought Roberto Escobar was surly and humorless, but his supervisor insisted that he was a good worker, and reliable until he'd failed to show up yesterday morning.

"So what if he ignores the other guys here, eats the lunch his wife sends instead of going out with them?" The balding, stringy man shrugged. After a moment, he added, "Maybe you can't tell me why you're looking for him, but... Will he be back to work?"

"I doubt it."

"So I'd better be replacing him." He was resigned, regretting the loss of a good worker but not the man.

Bruce's only glimmer of hope came from the last interview, when the middle-aged cashier said suddenly, "He did used to be friends with that other Mexican who worked here. Guy didn't speak much English. Uh... Pedro or José or one of those common names." She leaned back in her chair and opened the office door a crack. "Pete," she called, "you remember that Mexican used to work here? The one with the fake papers?"

"Yeah, yeah. Garcia."

"Carlos," she said with satisfaction. "Carlos Garcia. That's it. They talked during breaks. 'Course, no one else could understand a word they were saying."

"And this Garcia was the only person you noticed Roberto spending any time with?"

"Yeah, he wasn't a real friendly type. After Pete fired Carlos—and he about had to, once he found out his green card was fake—Roberto went back to sitting by himself at breaks. Couple months ago, we all went in together to buy flowers when Toby's wife died, but not Roberto. He was the only person working here who didn't contribute." The memory rankled, Bruce could tell.

Bank records next. Turned out the Escobars hadn't had a debit card. Roberto, Bruce learned, had been paid Thursday and deposited his check in the bank on the way home, all but two hundred dollars. No checks had cleared subsequently. Monday morning, Roberto in person had gone into his local branch office and withdrawn the entire amount. He'd also taken a cash advance against his one-and-only credit card—which, Bruce noted, had not had his wife's name on it. The whole added up to about fifteen hundred dollars. Not a lot, but if he had someplace to go where, even temporarily, he didn't have to pay rent, he'd have enough to get by for weeks, if not months.

Yeah, but how to find that place?

Still, the fact that he planned to need money was reassuring.

Uncle Mateo was up to talking this morning, although he broke down and cried every few minutes, his daughter and a daughter-in-law both fussing over him. Bruce hid how uncomfortable the display of raw emotion made him.

Uncle Mateo gave Bruce the names of a few men he thought might have been friends of Roberto's.

Yes, he'd suspected Roberto had hit Lenora sometimes, and since she had no father to speak for her, he had talked to her husband. Shaking his head, he said, "He thought it was his right. As if he were God inside his own house." He shook his head at the blasphemy of it.

God. Yes, that was a nice analogy. *King* was what Bruce's father had called himself. *If a man can't be king in his own castle...* That was one of his favorite lines, just after he backhanded his wife for being lippy—a cardinal sin in the Walker home—or committing any of a number of other sins. Or pulled out the leather belt to use on one of his sons.

As if paralleling Bruce's thoughts, Uncle Mateo begged, "What made him so crazy?"

Bruce wished he had an answer. Was it crazy? he wondered. Or too many years of being unchallenged? What would his own father have done if his wife had taken Bruce, Dan and Roger when they were little boys and fled? If a man was king, didn't he have the power of life and death over his subjects?

Knock it off, he ordered himself. It seemed every time he dealt with a certain form of domestic violence, he leaped like a hamster onto a wheel of useless bewilderment. Why, why, why? the wheel squeaked as it spun and went nowhere.

Damn it, he'd put it all behind him, except at moments like this. He detested this inability to stop himself from going back and attempting to reason out his own family history. He couldn't change the past; why replay it?

Back to see Karin Jorgensen. Lenora Escobar knew more about her husband than anyone, and he guessed that, in turn, she'd confided more in her counselor than she had in anyone else.

He called A Woman's Hand and, after waiting on hold for a couple of minutes, was told Karin would be free in an hour and would expect him. Glancing at his watch, he realized the free time would undoubtedly be her lunch break. He'd offer to feed them both.

The moment the receptionist spotted him, she picked up a phone. Karin came down the hall before he could reach the counter.

He hadn't imagined the tug he'd felt last night, even though exhaustion transformed her face from pretty to… Studying her, he struggled to understand. The only word he could come up with was *beautiful*. Not conventional, fashion-magazine beautiful, but something different: the purity old age or illness could bare when it stripped the illusions away and revealed the strength of bones and the life force beneath.

Bruce was not idiot enough to think she'd be flattered if he told her she looked beautiful like an old lady. And that wasn't exactly what he meant, anyway. It was more like seeing a woman in the morning without makeup for the first time, and realizing the crap she put on her face was not only unnecessary, but it blurred the clean lines.

Not that Bruce had ever thought any such thing upon seeing a woman's first-thing-in-the-morning face, but it seemed possible.

As she neared, Karin searched his eyes anxiously. "Have you heard anything about Lenora? Or found the children?"

He held out a hand, although he felt a surprising urge to hold out his arms, instead. "Last I knew, she's still unconscious. And no, regrettably."

"Oh." She put her hand in his, and seemed not to notice that he didn't shake it, only clasped it. Or perhaps she did because her fingers curled to hold his, as if she was grateful for the contact.

"Why don't we go get lunch," he suggested.

"Oh, that's a good idea. I suppose you don't usually take the time to stop."

"Drive-through at a burger joint is usually the best I do."

She shuddered. "I'm a vegetarian. Um...let me get my purse."

He waited patiently, although he had every intention of paying for the meal.

Every block of the nearby stretch of Madison Street had a choice of trendy bistros and cafés tucked between boutiques, gourmet pet food shops and art galleries. The shopping area was an extension of an area of pricey homes and condos, many with peekaboo views of Lake Washington and the skyline of Bellevue on the other side. The street itself dead-ended at the lake, where city-paid lifeguards presided over the beach in summer.

Bruce let Karin choose a place, and they sat outside on a little brick patio between buildings. Today was cool enough that they were alone out there, which was fine by him.

She ordered a salad, Bruce a heartier sandwich and bowl of soup. Then they sat and looked at each other while the waitress walked away.

"Are you all right?" he asked quietly.

She tried to smile. "A nap would do wonders. But you must have gotten even less sleep."

"I'm used to it. But that's not really what I meant."

"I know." She began to pleat her cloth napkin, her head bent as she appeared to concentrate on an elaborate origami project that wasn't creating anything recognizable to his eyes. "When Roberto hit her with the tire iron, it made an awful sound. I keep hearing…" For a second her fingers clenched instead of folding, then they relaxed and smoothed the damage to the napkin.

Bruce watched, as fascinated by her hands as she was.

"Naturally, I didn't sleep very well." She stole a glance up, her eyes haunted. "I saw him coming. And now I measure distances in my head and think, if I'd run, could I somehow have reached them in time?"

"You might have gotten your skull crushed, too," he said brutally. "Julia Lopez did her best to defend herself. Her forearm was shattered before a second blow hit her head."

"Ohh." Her fingers froze, and she stared at him. "Oh."

The image of her flinging herself between the furious, betrayed husband and the wife he was determined to kill shook Bruce. He tried not to let her see how much.

"There's no way you could have reached her in time anyway. Even if it had been physically possible, you would have had to read his intentions first, and that would have taken critical seconds."

"I should have walked her to the van."

"I repeat—unless you're trained in martial arts, you couldn't have done anything but get hurt."

Her shoulders sagged and the napkin dropped to her lap. "Do you think… Is there any way…?"

"She'll survive?"

Karin bit her lip and nodded.

"Of course it's possible." Why not? People had huge malignant tumors vanish between one ultrasound and the next. They woke from comas after twenty years. Miracles happened. "From what I've read, the brain has amazing recuperative properties. Other parts step in when one section is damaged. Right now, I'm guessing the swelling is what's keeping her in the coma."

Those big brown eyes were fixed on his face as if she were drinking in every word. She nodded. "That's what the doctor said."

"It takes time." He glanced up. "Ah. Here's our food."

They both ate, initially in a silence filled with undercurrents. He studied her surreptitiously, and caught her scrutinizing him, as well. He knew why she interested him so much. The question of the day: Did she see him only as a cop, or had it occurred to her to be intrigued by the man?

He cleared his throat. "I hope you weren't alone last night. Uh…this morning."

"Alone? No, Cecilia did sit with me for a while, and then Lenora's sister came…." Comprehension dawned. "Oh. You mean at home."

Bruce nodded.

"I live alone. I mean, I'm not married, or…"

Was that a blush, or was he imagining things?

"I fell into bed without even brushing my teeth. I was past coherent conversation."

He understood that. "I, ah, live alone, too."

"Oh." Definitely color in her cheeks, and her normally direct look skittered from his.

Well. They'd settled that. It was a start. Although to what he wasn't sure. He kept his relationships with women superficial, and somehow he didn't picture Karin Jorgensen being content with cheap wine when she could have full-bodied.

Great analogy; he was cheap.

No, not cheap—just not a keeper.

Somehow that didn't sound any better.

"The clinic's receptionist said you had questions for me."

He swallowed the bite of food in his mouth. *Clear your head, idiot.* "I want to know every scrap you can remember about Roberto Escobar. I'm hitting dead ends everywhere else I turn. No one liked him. I have a handful of names of men who might have been friends of his, although most people I've interviewed doubt he actually had any friends. If he really doesn't, if he's on his own with two little kids, we'll find him. If he has help, that's going to be tougher."

She set down her fork. "What do you think he'll do if he is on his own?"

"Rent a cheap motel room. Two hundred bucks a week. That kind."

Karin nibbled on her lower lip. "That sounds…bleak."

"It is bleak. Especially since I doubt he's ever done child care for more than a few hours at a time." He hadn't thought to ask anyone. "Is Enrico still in diapers?"

She shook her head. "Lenora was really happy to get him potty trained just…I don't know, six weeks or so ago. Although that isn't very long. Under stress, kids tend to regress."

She wasn't exaggerating. Under enough stress, they regressed by years sometimes. He'd seen a twelve-year-old curling up tightly and sucking her thumb. Having your mother brutally bludgeoned right in front of you… Yeah, that would be cause to lose bladder control.

"He'd be mad," Bruce noted.

"Oh, he'd be mad at them no matter what. Enrico is two. You know what two-year-olds are like."

He didn't, except by reputation.

"And Anna is only four. Well, almost five. They need routine, they need naps, they'll want their favorite toys—" She stopped. "Did he take the time to collect any of their stuff from their aunt and uncle's?"

"After killing Aunt Julia, you mean?" he said dryly. "We assume they had a bag packed for the night, and if so, yes. It's not there. But the ragged, stuffed bunny Uncle Mateo says Anna is passionately attached to was left on the sofa, along with Enrico's blankie. Uncle Mateo predicts major tears."

"Stupid," she pronounced.

"He panicked. Wouldn't you, under the circumstances?"

"Yes, but he'll be sorry." Then she shook her head,

visibly going into psychologist mode. "No, *sorry* isn't in his vocabulary. Not if it means, *Gee, I screwed up.* Everything is someone else's fault. The more he gets frustrated with the children, the more enraged he'll be at Lenora. This is all *her* fault. What's frightening is that without her to deflect him, he'll start turning that rage on Anna and Enrico. That he would anyway is worrying. That's what finally precipitated her decision to leave him. She knew that sooner or later he'd lose his temper with them, not just with her."

The sandwich was settling heavily in Bruce's stomach. He was hearing a professional opinion, professionally delivered. "How soon will that happen?"

"Soon. It probably already has. If he'd attacked just Lenora, I'd think there was a chance that he'd have a period of being…chilled. Justifying it in his own mind, but shaken by what he'd done, too. The fact that he attacked two women, with—what, fifteen minutes, half an hour in between?—suggests that he's even more cold-blooded than I would have guessed. No, he'll have very little patience. His own children are just…possessions to him. Evidence of his virility. Not living, breathing, squalling, traumatized kids. He literally has no ability to empathize."

Bruce swore. He supposed he had hoped Escobar was a man made momentarily insane by what he perceived as his wife's betrayal.

Ah, here we go again. Hamster wheel squeaking. What was true insanity—what was cultural and what was in the blood, a legacy from father to son?

Give me a straightforward murder for profit any day.

In this case, at least, Karin was telling him that Roberto Escobar wasn't momentarily nuts. He was the real thing: a genuine sociopath. One who, unfortunately, was on the run with two preschoolers. Now, *that* was scary.

He mined Karin for every tidbit she could dredge from her memory about her client's husband. His favorite color was red; Lenora had once mentioned looking for a shirt for his birthday. Did it say that the guy loved the color of blood?

"He's five foot eight, not five-ten as it says on his driver's license. Lenora said he lied."

Bruce made a note.

"He snores. But he didn't like it when she slipped out of bed to sleep on the couch or got in bed with one of the kids. So usually she didn't, even if she couldn't sleep."

Snores, he wrote, for no good reason. Unless someone in a cheap motel complained to the manager about a guy who sawed wood on the other side of the wall?

He noted food likes and dislikes, Roberto's opinion about people he worked with, his anger at what in his view was his mother's betrayal.

"Guy wasn't doing well where the women in his family were concerned," Bruce commented.

"No, and Lenora admitted to being inspired by the way his mother just let his words wash over her—like rain running over a boulder, I think is what she said—and kept on with her plans to go home to Mexico. Possibly for the first time, she realized he could be defied."

"I wonder if that was a good part of why he was so angry. Afraid his wife would see a chink in his supremacy?"

"Um…" She pursed her lips and thought about it. "No, I doubt he reasoned it out that well. Or believed Lenora had it in her to defy him in turn. Mostly, he'd have been angry that his mother chose her other son. Although since he's continued to call her, he may be channeling that anger onto his brother, who somehow lured their mother from her duty to her older son."

"In other words, he has a massively egocentric view of the world."

"Oh, entirely," Karin assured him.

They quibbled over the bill, with Bruce winning. He couldn't help noticing how little she'd actually eaten. He suspected she'd picked up her fork from time to time more to be unobtrusive about not eating than out of actual hunger.

While they walked back to the clinic, he called the hospital for an update on Lenora. "No change," he told Karin, pocketing his cell phone.

"I'll sit with her this evening, if they'll let me."

"Don't wear yourself out."

There was a flash of humor in her eyes when she glanced sidelong at him. "And you're not doing the same?"

"It's my job."

"Uh-huh. Don't I remember you saying, 'I'm taking this personally'?"

"It did piss me off that this bastard assaulted his wife damn near under my nose," he admitted.

"Was he watching when you walked away?" she wondered aloud.

"And did he know I was a cop?" He shrugged. "Hard to say. It was certainly luck on his part that Lenora was one of the last out of the building."

"If she hadn't stopped to talk to me…"

"Damn it." He gripped her elbow, stopping on the sidewalk in front of the clinic. "Don't keep trying to blame yourself. Talking to you was important to her."

They were facing each other, standing very close, staring into each other's faces. Her thick, long lashes, dark tipped with gold, were the perfect frame for her warm brown eyes. Without conscious volition, his gaze lowered to her mouth, and to the tiny mole beside it. He couldn't remember ever wanting to kiss a woman as desperately as he did this one. His head might have even dipped, before he saw again how worn and vulnerable she looked right now.

"God," he muttered, let go of her elbow and stepped back.

Her eyes seemed dilated, before a jolt shuddered through her and she blinked. "Oh. Um…" She drew in a deep breath and regained some poise, although he was afraid she'd shatter if car brakes squealed a block away. "Thank you for lunch."

"You're welcome," he said, voice rough. *Will you have dinner with me? Come home with me afterward?*

"Will you call me?" she asked.

For an instant, his hopes soared. Yes, she wanted to have dinner with him; she wanted… And then he crashed and burned. Not what she was asking. Not what she wanted.

Hiding his chagrin, he nodded. "I'll keep you informed."

"Okay." She backed away. "Thank you. Um, goodbye."

"I mean it. Take care of yourself. She may need you later. She doesn't yet."

Just before turning away, Karin said, "I think maybe *I* need her. Or at least to feel needed."

Who was he to tell a psychologist what she really felt or ought to feel?

Resigned, he shrugged and repeated, "I'll call," then went to his car, watching until she disappeared into A Woman's Hand before getting in and starting the engine.

Back to the hunt, before the trail he followed grew cold.

CHAPTER FOUR

THE REST OF THE DAY was more of the same. Bruce mostly left the Lopez house to the crime scene people. His driving interest was in finding Roberto. Clues to where he'd disappeared with the children wouldn't be at the Lopez house.

Instead, Bruce returned to Escobar's own house and walked through it again, trying to soak in details. The entire while he was conscious of the need to be there, but also felt unpleasantly like an intruder. Lenora wasn't dead—not yet, at least. That made the house still a home in a sense, rather than a crime scene.

The place was spotless except for the messes Roberto had made over the weekend—unwashed dishes and the damage left by his fury. Did both Roberto and Lenora believe cleanliness was next to godliness? Or was Lenora such a scrupulous housekeeper because her husband insisted on it?

He'd have to ask Karin what she thought. Not that it probably mattered, except that a cop never knew what insight might later prove relevant.

No, use your own judgment. Karin isn't here. He couldn't be calling her incessantly.

Okay, then. The way soup cans were aligned in kitchen cupboards, shoes were in neat rows by pairs in the closets, unused possessions carefully boxed and labeled on shelves was not the mark of an unwilling housekeeper. Even the kids' bedroom, shared, had to have been clean and well organized before Roberto had ripped clothes from drawers and hangers in impatience.

Bruce found a box of romance novels tucked in the linen closet behind stacks of sheets and pillowcases, where Roberto would likely never have seen it. They were fairly recent ones, with a stamp inside the cover from a nearby used bookstore. So Lenora was still able to dream, and not necessarily about her husband. Did Karin know she read these, or was Lenora secretly embarrassed about this escape? Bruce felt a savage wish that she'd have the chance to dream again.

The fourth or fifth time he speculated on what Karin would think about this habit or that room, he growled. What was wrong with him? He didn't lose confidence in his judgment every time he worked with someone better educated than he was.

No, the problem was, he couldn't get her out of his head. And because she was along for the ride, so to speak, he had this bizarre desire to talk to her. Better yet, for her to talk back.

The realization disturbed him. He was single-minded in the hours and days after a murder. He forgot to eat, or to taste the food if he did remember. He did not—repeat, *did not*—keep thinking about a woman.

As if in defiance, he found himself picturing her.

She'd be nearing the end of her day, maybe in with her last client. He had no trouble seeing how she'd listen with grave interest, her attention wholly and flatteringly on the speaker. His inner eye lingered on the line of her throat, her golden-blond hair bundled heavy at her nape.

What is it with her neck, anyway? Okay, I'll think about her lips, instead. Or her eyes, the color of melted chocolate. No, her lips. Or...both.

"Crap!" Scowling, he stalked out of the house, less than happy to have thoughts of a woman riding him quite so hard. Yeah, it *had* been a while since he'd been in a relationship, so it wasn't surprising he was so hot for this one. But the *combination*—wanting her and wanting to discuss with her everything that passed through his mind—that made him uneasy.

His brooding was interrupted by a call letting him know that the blood on the tire iron did in fact come from two separate individuals, confirmed to be Lenora Escobar and Julia Lopez. Time of death on the aunt further corroborated that she'd died first. So the kids presumably were in the car at the time of their mother's assault. Appalled, Bruce hoped they'd been clutching each other in the back seat, not even watching when their daddy got out. Wouldn't they have screamed or called out if they'd seen their mother?

Maybe they had and no one heard them.

Whether they could see out the window depended on whether they'd been in their car seats and therefore sat tall enough. Bruce shook his head. He'd forgotten to check on where the kids' car seats were. He made a note now.

Neither woman who witnessed the crime had observed the car. Bruce would like to think that meant it wasn't in sight. From previous experience, however, he suspected that their gazes had been riveted on Lenora.

Damn it, he wanted confirmation that Escobar *had* been driving his own vehicle. Yeah, it was missing; yeah, both Cecilia and Karin had identified Lenora's assailant as Roberto from a family photo Mateo Lopez had supplied. But at this point, finding him depended on finding his car. If he'd switched—borrowed a different one, stolen one—God, owned a second one that hadn't yet been registered?—then escape became more possible.

To clear his head, Bruce called Molly, and learned that her new niece was enchanting, adorable and had lungs the size and power of an opera singer's.

"Murder sounds good," she said a little wistfully. "But I promised to stay until Thursday, when Mom is flying in. I *told* her Fiona was the size of a house and I thought the baby would come sooner than next week, but who listens to me?"

The question was clearly rhetorical, so Bruce didn't comment. Molly's mother had found a second career leading groups on tours and was currently in the Ozarks. Since it was a one-woman business, she couldn't abandon her group.

"This is an ugly one," Bruce said, instead. "The bastard was willing to kill two women out of pride. He couldn't let his wife leave him and take his children."

"Hmm. And he grabbed the kids first, you say? Did he

go intending to kill the aunt? Or was he just thinking he had the right to take his children and she'd stand aside?"

"Kill." Bruce didn't have much doubt. "I guess it's conceivable he went to the door first and they argued, but then you'd think the aunt would have locked up in the time it took him to go back to his car, pop the trunk and grab the tire iron. He didn't have to break in, and it's hard to imagine she'd have opened the door to him a second time. The family wasn't fond of Roberto."

"Son of a bitch," she muttered. "Maybe Fiona can find a friend who'd stay with her tomorrow."

"No. Enjoy your niece. Catch up on your sleep. I've pulled in plenty of help."

She snorted. "Catch up on my sleep. Yeah. Right. You should *hear* this kid."

"And someday you, too, will have one of your own," he told her, grinning. "Or two or three… Hey, five or six, you being Catholic and all."

She said something rude that left him laughing as he ended the call.

It was getting on to the dinner hour, perfect for catching people at home, so he tried the addresses for two of the names he'd been given as potential friends of Escobar's. No answer when Bruce knocked at the first, an apartment. At the second, he talked to Ramiro Payeda against the din of half a dozen children squabbling at the table while his wife tried to keep them focused on eating their dinner.

"*Amigos?*" Payeda said doubtfully. Well, he *knew* Escobar, sure. They had worked together previously.

He explained that they'd both moonlighted from their regular jobs with a weekend roofing crew. Roberto had gotten a raise at the lumberyard and quit the second job. Payeda hadn't seen him in at least a year.

Another dead end. Bruce thanked him for his time and left.

It was now eight in the evening. The blue of the sky was taking on deeper tones. Good. Time to recanvass the neighbors up and down the street from A Woman's Hand. Some had either not been home or hadn't answered their doors last night. A second round today had caught a few of those at home, but none who'd heard the squealing tires or noticed a speeding vehicle. This was the perfect time of night to get the last few.

Once again, cars were wedged in every available spot along the street. Street parking was at a premium. Many of these older homes had narrow driveways and single-car, detached garages. He left his own car in the clinic lot, pausing only momentarily where the bloodstain was still evident. He'd noticed when he picked up Karin for lunch how careful she'd been not to look that way as they'd walked out. It would be a long time before she could come to work and not think about what happened. Like the victims she counseled, she would never feel quite as safe again.

Bruce checked his list of who had been interviewed and who hadn't, and went to the first door. The porch light came on, and a gray-haired, paunchy guy opened the door.

Last night? No, he and his wife had had dinner at their daughter's and hadn't gotten home until about eleven. Missed the excitement, although they'd heard about it from neighbors. Sorry.

No answer still at the next place.

At the third on his list, two houses down from A Woman's Hand, a man in his thirties answered the doorbell. He wore a uniform, and raised his brow in surprise when Bruce held out his badge.

"Cop, huh? I work security for Reliant. I'm on the night shift. I was just finishing dinner."

"Sorry to interrupt it," Bruce said. He explained his errand.

The guy was nodding before he finished. "Yeah, this jerk parked right in front of my driveway last night. I went out to go to work, and I could tell I wouldn't be able to get out. I'd gone in to call for a tow truck, when I looked out the window and saw him come running. He jumped in, did a U-turn, bumped over the curb across the street and just missed a parked car—" he nodded that way "—and then was gone."

Bruce flipped open his notebook. "Can you describe the vehicle?"

He could and did. Aging Buick, medium blue, must get shit for mileage, some rust on the right side door, dented front fender.

Without having written down the license plate number, he couldn't have more accurately described Roberto Escobar's car.

He hadn't heard screams. He'd presumably been inside during and immediately after the assault. Also, he admitted with some embarrassment, he'd had his iPod on. Shortly after the car sped away, he'd gone out again and left for work.

Bruce confirmed the time of the incident and had him describe the man he'd seen to the best of his ability. *Bingo.* Bruce took down his name and thanked him. "You've been a big help."

So. At least they now knew they were looking for the right car. That was something. Not enough, but something.

Back in his own car, undecided about his next move, Bruce thumped his fist on the steering wheel. How in hell had someone like Escobar gone so successfully to ground? However cold-blooded he was, he had to have been rattled. And, damn it, he was towing two preschool-age kids along with him!

Short of driving by cheap motels himself, Bruce couldn't think of a single other thing he could do tonight. He hated hitting this moment in an investigation. Ideally, the bastard should be behind bars by now. Failing that accomplishment, Bruce wanted to keep working. He was still on hyperdrive. He detested this sense that every direction he turned he banged into a blank wall.

I could go by the hospital.

Uh-huh. And that served what purpose? He'd have gotten a call if Lenora Escobar had either died or stunned everyone by opening her eyes and asking where she was and what had happened.

It was nine o'clock. Chances were Karin had gone home by now, even if she had indeed spent part of the evening sitting with Lenora.

Still. He could find out, couldn't he? Talking to her might quell this restlessness.

He'd started the car and was driving before he had consciously made a decision.

Any excuse to see Karin Jorgensen again.

KARIN SAT in a dreamlike state, her hand on Lenora's. The beep and hum of monitors were oddly comforting, a mother's "Sh, it's all right" murmur translated to a technological age.

Karin knew better, of course. A steady heartbeat, air pushed in and out of lungs meant nothing if Lenora's brain never regained conscious function.

The swelling was subsiding, doctors said. She wasn't brain dead. There were reflexes.

Karin had to take their word on faith. The hand beneath hers was utterly still. Her monologue awakened no response.

Maybe because she wasn't saying what Lenora needed desperately to hear: *We've found the children. They're fine.* Instead, inspiration at a low ebb, she'd been talking about the weather and how she loved spring.

"I'm turning into a gardener," she said. "Did I ever tell you that? It's funny, because I used to roll my eyes when my mother went outside and spent hours and hours grubbing in the dirt. When I was about fifteen, I'd be embarrassed if I had friends over to our house and Mom would come in sweating and filthy and triumphant because the trillium had appeared. 'They're hard to establish, you know,' she'd say. She showed me the three trilliums that had popped up, and they were these funny little plants on a thin stalk with three leaves at the top. Not what you'd call a thriller." She laughed softly, although given the time and place, there was very little humor in the sound. "But me, I wasn't interested. Until I bought a condo, and every year I filled a few more pots with annuals. I knew I was in trouble when I took a class at a nursery so my flower baskets would be unusual instead of just cheerful, with the usual geraniums or pansies. And then I bought a house, and it was all downhill. It looked so *bare* under the trees in the backyard, and I thought, *Just a few woodland plants*. Then the lawn in front and the single flowering cherry tree weren't that interesting. So I dug out a bed along the fence. I have a white picket fence. Hmm. There must be something psychological in that, do you think?" She paused as if for answer, but didn't need one. Yes, indeedy, there was something psychological in the classic symbol of home: a white picket fence. "Anyway," she continued into the silence that lay beneath the sounds of the hospital, "now I'm digging out two more beds to each side of the front porch. I've gotten hooked on old roses, and I want room for more. The worst part? When I got excited this spring because my trillium had spread in back. I called Mom—she lives in Portland— and begged forgiveness for every time I sneered. Mom just laughed."

Maybe this wasn't the best topic, she thought, disconcerted. Because in the end, her story had been about family and home, and not plants or spring as she'd intended. But maybe it was okay, because she wasn't talking about children, which she did not have, and which to Lenora had been all important.

Karin would have left Roberto the first time he'd hit her. But then, she wasn't poor, uneducated and just delivered of her first baby. She had options Lenora had never had.

Options Karin had wanted so much to give her.

"Should I have encouraged you?" she whispered. "You knew him. I didn't. I just…guessed."

And had been frightened, she reminded herself. She'd had that much sense.

She remembered a wistful voice: *I wish we could join the witness protection program or something like that.*

What had she told Lenora in return? Oh, yes. *Just disappear.*

Was that what Lenora had done, faced with the unbearable? There was more than one way to disappear.

A throat cleared behind her. "Hey."

Startled, she turned.

Detective Bruce Walker stood a few feet from the bed, seeming to fill the cubicle with his broad shoulders and tough presence. His posture was relaxed, his gaze resting thoughtfully on her face.

She felt a flush creep over her cheeks. How long had he been standing there? "Um… Have you been eavesdropping on my inane chatter?"

"I heard something about trillium," he admitted. "And then you whispered."

"The whispering part I should have left out." She squeezed Lenora's hand, which could have belonged to a mannequin. "Lenora shouldn't be worrying, not now. She has to concentrate on getting better."

He nodded and stepped closer to the side of the bed, where he wrapped his hands around the metal railing and said, "Hi, Lenora. Bruce Walker. I'm the guy who taught the self-defense workshop. I'm…feeling pretty bad that I didn't say anything that would have helped you. But you're going to defeat Roberto by opening your eyes and by walking into court to testify against him. You're going to be one of the lucky women who sees your abuser sent to prison for a long time. So long you'll be able to quit worrying about him. Feel safe. Raise your kids. That's the ending we're waiting for, when your head quits hurting the way it does."

Karin stared at him. How did he do that—say the right thing so effortlessly? She'd been tiptoeing all around the assault, not wanting to upset the unconscious woman if she was making sense of any of the words spoken to her. But this cop had in essence told her, *Survive and you win.* What could be a more important message to send?

He lifted his gaze and studied Karin. "It's getting late. Have you been here all evening?"

"Oh, not that long." Almost, but what else was she supposed to do? Go home and watch sitcoms? "Yolanda spent most of the day here. I made her leave. Her husband and kids need her, too."

He nodded acknowledgment. "Why don't you say good-night," he suggested. "I'll buy you a cup of coffee on your way out. Or warm milk—" a smile crinkled his eyes "—depending on how quickly you want to hit the sack."

Her answering smile took more effort than she'd thought she had it in her to make. "Warm milk it is, then." She stood, her knees protesting, and bent to kiss Lenora's thin cheek just above the tube carrying oxygen. "He's right, Lenora. I'd better get some sleep so I can give my best to my clients in the morning. I'll come back tomorrow night. I hope by then you can interrupt me when my stories drag on too long."

She waited just a fraction of a second, unable to quell her human faith that someone who looked so alive must be listening. Then she gave what she knew to be an awkward little nod, picked up her purse and walked out.

She said good-night to the nurses, who smiled and assured her that her company had been important to the patient.

Only if she could hear me.

Once through the swinging doors that separated the hushed ICU from the rest of the hospital, Bruce said, "Trillium?"

She loved his voice. It had gravel in it, not so much as to make him sound like someone who'd had his throat damaged; no, just enough to make her toes curl. As if she was going to walk barefoot across him? Through him?

Beside him?

Now, why did that last thought make her shiver?

"The cafeteria should still be open," he said, taking her arm as if he'd done it a hundred times already and steering her to the left, rather than straight down the corridor. "I doubt a cup of coffee will do more than keep you awake long enough for you to make it safely home."

She suspected he was right. She just hoped sleep didn't elude her tonight, too. "You know your way around the hospital. I suppose the cafeteria here is your home away from home."

"One of 'em," he agreed.

They got coffee. Karin shook her head when he took a cinnamon roll and looked inquiringly at her. He insisted on paying, as he had at lunchtime.

The dining room was deserted except for a clearly weary couple who sat at a table near the window, eating but not conversing, their gazes turned inward. They were numb, she thought. Neither even glanced over when Bruce and Karin scraped chairs back from a table.

"Did you have dinner?" he asked with a frown.

"Dinner?" She had to think. "I went home and changed clothes." She indicated her chinos and sweater. "I stuck some vegetables and cream cheese in a pita. What about you?"

"Uh…" He couldn't answer because he was wolfing down the sticky bun.

"Honestly." She shook her head. "They had salads in that glass case."

"I didn't realize I was so hungry. If you don't mind waiting…?" He sounded sheepish.

She tried to assume a stern expression.

His mouth tilted up, and he went back into the cafeteria.

While he was gone, Karin sipped coffee, grateful

he'd stopped by. He was the one person she wanted most to see and talk to right now. Jerlyn, the mother figure at A Woman's Hand, had stopped her earlier and said quietly, "If you want to talk, day or night, you know where to find me." But Karin hadn't felt any impulse to spill her powerfully suppressed turmoil to Jerlyn, no matter how much she usually valued her input. This time, she would simply have to live with the guilt and second thoughts and, oh, memory of that terrible sound.

But she couldn't deny that she kept trying to spill her anguish to the man who wended his way back between tables with a tray that held a wrapped sub, a salad and, yes, another cinnamon roll. And each time he just nodded, unsurprised, making her realize he'd heard it all before, probably *felt* it all before. And that was why she felt so comfortable with him. His life was like hers in that he would have had no job were it not for other people's tragedies. Only, he saw those tragedies one step closer. The psychological aftereffects were her vocation, the physical his.

Sitting down, he unwrapped the sandwich. "So. Trillium?"

"It's a flower."

"I vaguely knew that. Why did it make your mother laugh?"

Then he'd arrived at the end of her monologue, not the beginning.

So Karin told the silly, but no doubt deeply revealing, story again, and enjoyed his smile at the end.

"You need a T-shirt. 'I'm my mother.'"

She made a face at him. "Are you your father?"

Something closed on his face. Bang! Sealed like a vault. "God, I hope not."

What had his father *done* to make him sound so appalled? Would it be an awful intrusion if she asked?

He swallowed and met her eyes, his face still expressionless, and she had her answer. *Yes.*

So she bit her lip. "I assume you didn't come tonight to tell me you'd found Roberto and the kids."

He grimaced. "No such luck. I do know now that he was still driving his own car when he attacked Lenora. And, uh, that he did use the tire iron on both Julia and Lenora."

She took that in. "Then the children almost had to be in the car."

"Yes, but now I know where he parked it while he assaulted his wife. Anna and Enrico couldn't have seen what happened."

"Oh." Her voice failed, and she whispered, "Thank God."

He was watching her. Seeming satisfied, he said, "Otherwise, I'm stymied. Where the hell is he?"

She shook her head and cradled the coffee cup in her hands.

"I kept thinking about you today." He still appeared relaxed, his long legs outstretched under the table, but there was something not quite happy in his voice.

"In a bad way?"

"Huh? Oh. No. Just wondering what you'd say about

this, how you'd read that. If you can get into his head better than I can."

Absurd to feel disappointed. What else had she thought he meant? That he'd been mooning over her?

"I think," she admitted, "that I get into women's heads better than men's. Which might be why I'm un-married and, well, unattached." Now, why had she said that? Did she want to sound pathetic? "You have an ad-vantage over me where Roberto's concerned."

At her revelation, his eyes had narrowed, just for a beat. But he let that go. "Maybe, but I have a problem where Roberto's concerned."

"What do you mean?"

"He reminds me unpleasantly of my father, which makes it hard for me to evaluate him dispassionately."

Oh. That was why he'd hated the idea that he might be like his father. Considering how little he'd wanted to talk about it, just a minute earlier, she was left wonder-ing why he'd chosen to bring the subject up now.

She judged that sympathy wasn't what he wanted. So she said only, "To find Roberto, do you have to understand in what ways he might be different from your father?"

He cracked the plastic top from the salad and frowned down at it. "If I know him better, I can take more accurate guesses at what he'd do in any given circum-stance. He's smart, or we'd have found him by now."

She nodded. "He thinks more clearly than most of us would under similar stress. Rage and pride are his primary emotions. But Lenora used to talk about how he'd blow up, beat her and then walk away calmly, as if nothing had happened. He'd turn on the TV, tell her to bring him a beer, call his mother. In his view, nothing *had* happened, because he couldn't empathize with her fear or pain."

"So, cold and careful, except when he's in the midst of a rage." He shook his head. "No wonder everybody disliked him."

"I suspect it was the coldness that made them uneasy. We unconsciously look for signals from other people, appropriate responses to what we're saying or doing. He wouldn't be giving them."

Bruce abruptly pushed away the barely touched salad. "Come on. Let's get out of here. You must be beat."

"Gee, thanks."

His gaze flicked to her face, and there was sudden heat in his eyes. "You're the most beautiful exhausted woman I've ever seen."

He might as well have zapped her with a lightning bolt. Her blood heated, and her lower belly cramped with longing. She couldn't look away from that glint in his eyes.

She'd known, of course, that she found him attractive. But she'd been distracted enough not to react sexually. He'd just changed that. Karin wasn't sure how she felt about that. She was unnerved enough to regain a semblance of self-control.

"Thank you again. I guess."

He gave a gruff laugh. "Not the prettiest compliment you've ever heard, is it?"

"Well, no, but…"

"But?"

Neither of them had moved. He hadn't picked up his tray.

"The thought was nice." Not what she'd meant to say, but it would do. How could she ask, *Did you mean it? Do you really think I'm beautiful?*

He nodded, picked up his tray and started for the exit. The subject was apparently closed. She waited while he took care of the tray, then walked beside him down the deserted hall.

"Where's your car?" he asked.

She told him, not bothering to insist she didn't need an escort. For one thing, tonight, she was very glad to have one. For another… *Admit it.* She didn't want to say good-night. She didn't know when she'd see him again.

They were in the parking garage when he said, "If I invited you to dinner, would you say yes?"

Karin hadn't felt a clutch of excitement like this in years. She shouldn't now. She made a point of not dating men who were as steeped in the violent underside of human nature as she was. But she had the oddest flash of revelation. How had she expected to fall in love with someone she couldn't talk to?

She must have been quiet too long, because he continued, "If my invitation makes you uncomfortable, say so. We'll consider the subject closed."

"Yes," she said. "I mean, no. I mean…"

He stopped and faced her. Around them, the garage

was brightly lit, yet somehow shadowy. They were very much alone.

"Yes? Or no?"

"Yes," she whispered. "I'd say yes."

There was that look in his eyes again, the one that seemed to liquefy her. "Good," he murmured. "When we have time…"

Her head bobbed. *Soon, please.*

He touched her cheek, brushing it with his knuckles, so softly a shiver passed down her spine.

"What is it about you?" he said, so quietly she knew the question wasn't meant for her.

But then he let his hand drop. "You should get home before you collapse. Where's the car?"

"Um…there at the end."

Hand gripping her arm, he led her to her Camry, then waited while she fumbled in her purse, found her keys and unlocked the driver's-side door. "You'll be okay?"

"I don't live five minutes from here. You'd better go home and get some sleep, too." A smile came from nowhere, surprising her. "Although you're the sexiest exhausted man I've ever seen."

He laughed, as she'd meant him to.

"Yeah, I think I can sleep now. Thanks."

Thanks for what? she wondered, getting into her car. Listening to him? Persuading him to eat? Or flirting with him?

"Do you want a lift to your car?"

"Nah, I'm not far away."

"Then good night."

"Good night."

By the time she backed out, he was striding off. She was only a little sorry he hadn't kissed her. There would be a better time.

CHAPTER FIVE

BRUCE JACKKNIFED UP in bed, lit numbers on his clock a reproach. Oh, crap! He'd forgotten to call Trevor.

At after one in the morning, it was too late now. Feeling guilty, he lay back down. Damn it, what if MaryBeth hadn't come home in the day and a half since he'd dropped off Trev? What if the cupboards were bare? Who was it Trevor had said checked on him "sometimes"? Mrs. Potter? No, Porter. Mrs. Porter. Would he feel okay about going to her if he didn't have any food?

He could've called me, Bruce reminded himself. He had Bruce's cell phone number.

Question is, would he if he wasn't desperate? Trevor tried very hard to pretend he and his mom were doing fine. He wouldn't want to admit they weren't.

Bruce eventually quieted his restless conscience enough to sleep. But Wednesday morning when he called Trevor, he got no answer. Frowning, he thought about driving over there, except by the time he reached White Center, Trev should be on the school bus.

Later.

Still no change in Lenora's condition when he

phoned the hospital. Bruce set out to find more of the men who might have been friends of Roberto's, with no luck. Midday he had word that a pair of uniformed cops, visiting a run-down motel on a tip that a drug dealer was there, had spotted a car that might be Escobar's. Wrong plates, but the ones on the car had been stolen or borrowed from a red 1972 Chevy pickup. This vehicle was a LeSabre, blue, rusting, dented. They hadn't gotten too close because they'd seen the curtain twitch. Should they move on it?

He had them watch the hotel-room door and wait for him. He drove fast, his adrenaline pumping. It was about time they got lucky. Man, he hoped those kids were okay.

"I don't think he has a gun," he told the young cop who was waiting when he got there. "But let's not count on it."

The cop nodded. He and his partner had extracted the key to the room from the manager, and the partner had stayed in the office to be sure the manager didn't call to warn his tenant.

The two of them walked down the row of rooms, smelling marijuana seeping from one room, hearing a dog scrabbling and whining in another. Most of the cars parked out front were beaters. A couple of the rooms had junk heaped on the sidewalk, people moving in or out or maybe partway and losing interest.

The uniform arranged himself on the opposite side of the door from Bruce, his weapon in his hand. Bruce hammered on the door.

"Police! Open up."

Inside something scrabbled, much like the dog, but this time Bruce sensed the sound was made by a human.

He wasn't giving Escobar long enough to kill the kids. He pounded again, yelling, "Open the door now or we're coming in."

Silence. He had the key in the lock when the door abruptly swung inward under his hand.

A skinny, pasty, pimply kid peered out, looking scared. "Whaddya want? We haven't done anything!"

Shit.

"Open the door wide," Bruce ordered.

It swung open to reveal four other teenagers, ranging at his best guess from thirteen up to maybe seventeen. Runaways. Goddamn it, runaways! Not Escobar.

"Is that your vehicle?" he asked, nodding over his shoulder at the Buick.

"It's mine," one of the girls said defiantly. "What's it to you? I'm not even driving it!"

"Plates are stolen."

"They're from my car," a boy said. "It won't start, and I can't afford to get it fixed."

"And I couldn't afford the tabs," the girl said. "So big deal. What's his and mine is ours."

Goddamn, Bruce thought again. He shook his head. "We're going to have to check you all out. Someone will be wanting to know where you are."

"I won't stay in no shelter!" a scrawny, wild-eyed girl said. "We paid for this place. We got a right."

Depressed, he left them to the custody of the two uniformed officers. Yeah, the kids probably weren't hurting anyone or anything except themselves. The girls would be turning tricks. Hell, maybe the boys, too. And all of them would be buying drugs when they could afford 'em. This at an age when they should be in middle school or high school, maybe working the counter at Burger King weekends for enough bucks to pay to take a girl out or buy the clothes Mom and Dad wouldn't spring for. Seeing kids like these upset him more than almost anything on the job, including dead bodies.

While he was out on this stretch of the Pacific Highway, he checked out a dozen similar motels, driving around back of each to be sure the rusting blue Buick wasn't tucked out of sight.

At three o'clock his cell phone rang. He pulled into the parking lot of a McDonald's and grabbed the phone from his belt.

"Walker."

"Bruce?" The voice was thin and boyish. "It's Trevor."

"Trev. I tried to call you this morning."

"I didn't hear the phone. I left early so I could, like, walk down to a different bus stop."

"Jackson?"

"He punched me yesterday!" The boy sniffed. "But everyone else at the stop said if I told, they'd say I just walked into a street sign."

Bruce ground his teeth. "You can't be the only kid he's bullying."

"I guess not." He sounded…uninterested, and Bruce tensed. If Trev hadn't phoned because of the bully at the bus stop…

"It's Mom!" the boy exclaimed. "She hasn't been home since Sunday."

"Sunday?" he echoed. "Damn it, Trevor, why didn't you say something? Have you had anything to eat?"

"At first there was stuff. And I get a hot lunch at school. So I was okay. Mom's gone sometimes for a day or two, but never this long. I'm scared!" His voice cracked and then rose. "Why hasn't she come home or called or anything?"

"I don't know. You sit tight. I'm on my way."

Obviously crying, the boy snuffled and said, "Right now?"

"Right now. It'll take me about fifteen minutes."

While he drove, he radioed in to find out if MaryBeth DeShon had been picked up and was in jail or detox, or if any unidentified bodies meeting her description had been found this week. "No" was the answer all around. Later, he'd make multiple calls to be sure she hadn't ended up in some other jurisdiction. Not for the first time, he wished the patchwork of cities and counties shared information better.

In the meantime… Damn it, what was he going to do with Trevor? Bruce wished like hell a responsible neighbor lived nearby, or the boy had a good friend with whom he could stay.

He'd no sooner knocked and called, "Trevor, it's me, Bruce," than his Little Brother flung open the door. He'd tried to scrub signs of tears from his face, but it was still blotchy, his eyes puffy.

Bruce stepped in and drew the boy, unresisting, to

him for a hug. No reason he should feel such anguish; the kid was okay.

Against his chest, Trevor repeated, "Mom and me— we're usually okay." He stiffened and stepped away, as if needing to regain his pride.

"I checked with hospitals to make sure she wasn't in an accident." He didn't say *or overdosed.* "She didn't look so good to me the last couple of times I saw her."

Trev's gaze slid from his. "I think maybe she's, I don't know, doing something different. 'Cuz it used to be she just drank and partied. You know. But now she gets real shaky right before she goes out. And…and I think she got fired from her job again last week."

MaryBeth had her shortcomings, but she'd done her damnedest to give her son a better childhood than she'd had. Would she have just walked? Everyone had a breaking point. Maybe she'd reached hers.

"I'm going to have to call Child Protective Services," Bruce said. "So you have someplace safe to stay, just while we hunt for her."

Trevor backed away, his eyes widening. "You mean, like a foster home? Can't I stay with you? I thought… when you said you were coming…"

Bruce shook his head. "You know what kind of hours I work. I'm home only to sleep."

"I can take care of myself!" the boy pleaded. "Mom practically always works nights I'm real responsible! That's what she says."

Bruce wavered, but only momentarily. He couldn't let himself get pulled two ways, feeling he should be home when he needed to be on the job. Homicide wasn't an eight-to-five gig.

"I believe you're responsible, but you're also twelve years old. You *shouldn't* be home alone a lot, and especially not at night. Your mom has done the best she could. I'm not criticizing her. But right now, you need stability, not another empty apartment."

Trevor backed away from him, his expression of disbelief morphing into anger. "You don't want me, do you? Just say so! Don't lie to me!"

Bruce's bad case of heartburn wouldn't be cured by a gulp of antacid. "If I had a different kind of job, or a wife who's there when I'm not, I'd like nothing better than to take you home with me. But I'm a homicide cop, and right now I'm looking for two kids who may be in danger. I can't let up, Trevor."

"I wish I hadn't called you," the boy said with loathing. "I shoulda just waited for Mom." With one hand he dashed furiously at his tears.

Bruce tried talking to him some more. The boy wouldn't listen. Doing his best to harden his heart, Bruce called CPS and requested a caseworker.

He offered to help Trevor pack while they waited, but the boy said, "I don't want you touching my stuff!" and slammed the bedroom door in Bruce's face.

He stood outside for a minute, rubbing his chest above the burning sensation, second-guessing himself. Did he know anyone who would be good for Trevor? But Molly had the same problem he did, plus she was helping her sister out with the newborn. Other fellow cops were single like him; or they had families, and how could he saddle them with an extra? He imagined how gentle Karin would be with him, but she needed to be with Lenora when she wasn't working.

Shaking his head finally, Bruce turned away from the closed door and wandered the apartment. With an effort, he forced himself to think like a cop. Had Trevor tried to determine whether his mother had packed enough to suggest she'd meant to be gone for more than a day or two?

Not sure if he'd be able to tell, Bruce quietly stepped into her bedroom. It was messy and smelled like unwashed armpits. Mattress on the floor, unmade bed-clothes, sheets stained. Another sheet was nailed up to cover the window. Cheap, pressboard dresser and a few hangers in the closet held what few clothes she owned or had left behind. In one corner, the kind of net hamper designed for dorm rooms was half full of dirty laundry, a bra hanging out. A couple of pairs of scuffed shoes, worn at the heels, were left where she'd kicked them off. He eased open the drawers one by one and found drug paraphernalia in the top one. Surprise, surprise.

No suitcase, but chances were she didn't own one. When she and her son moved, their possessions would go in grocery sacks and cardboard boxes from the state liquor store.

Her cosmetics littered the counter in the bathroom, which was dirty enough to make Bruce disinclined to touch anything. In the cup beside the sink were two toothbrushes, both needing replacement. He nudged open the medicine cabinet and saw a half-used foil packet of birth control pills. *Huh.* No, it didn't appear MaryBeth had intended to be gone long.

He was back out in the living room by the time the doorbell rang. The woman he let in had to be fresh out of college, but maybe that was all to the good. Her zeal wouldn't have been ground down to cynicism yet. She introduced herself as Caroline Connelly and asked how long it had been since Trevor's mother had been home.

Trev emerged from the bedroom while they talked, carrying his bulging book bag and a couple of plastic grocery sacks holding clothes. His face was set and pale, and he refused to look at Bruce.

The social worker introduced herself and gave an upbeat, everything-will-be-great speech that made him hunch his shoulders and stare at the floor. Finally, she said, "Do you have everything you need?"

He shrugged.

"Toothbrush?" Bruce reminded him.

Without a word, Trevor went into the bathroom, then returned a moment later.

"Why don't you set down your stuff and write a note to your mom," she suggested. "We'll tape it up where she can't miss it when she gets home."

Again, Trev complied without deigning to speak to Bruce. He pulled a lined sheet of paper from his pack and wrote on it in big letters: *Mom, when you didn't come home, they took me away to a foster home. You got to call to find out where I am.*

He wrote down the phone number Caroline Connelly gave him, then signed the note *Sorry, Trev.*

At Bruce's suggestion, Trevor called his neighbor, Mrs. Porter, and told her where he was going. Hearing only the one end, Bruce gathered she wasn't surprised.

"You'll actually be going to a receiving home," the social worker told him. "You might like that better, because you'll be with a bunch of other boys."

He stiffened. "Are they my age?"

"Twelve to fifteen."

He gave Bruce one desperate, despairing side glance. A sense of helplessness clawed at Bruce, who knew what torture school had become for Trevor this past year or two because the other boys were maturing physically faster than him. And while in some respect all the kids in the receiving home would be, like Trevor, victims of family dysfunction, many would already have been considerably toughened by their lives. Trevor was childlike and naive in contrast to many of the kids who were in and out of receiving and group homes.

Bruce said nothing until they'd locked the apartment and walked down to the cars, then spoke in an undertone to the social worker. "I think he'd do better in a foster home with some one-on-one—"

She was shaking her head before he'd gotten halfway through with what he'd wanted to say. "I don't have one available, not for a boy his age."

"But look at him."

She did, and he saw the dismay on her face she'd been trying to hide. But she only shook her head again.

Trevor put his stuff in the back seat, then got into the

front on the passenger side. Bruce laid a hand on the door before he could slam it.

"We'll find your mom."

He shrugged and ducked his head.

"I'll be in touch."

Trevor didn't say anything. Nor did his head turn when Caroline backed out and drove away.

Standing there, Bruce felt like scum.

KARIN WANDERED her living room, straightening magazines on the coffee table, fluffing the pillows on the sofa, refolding a throw before laying it carefully over the back of a chair. She wasn't, she realized, suffering from anxious-hostess syndrome so much as she was trying to keep herself occupied.

What on earth had she been thinking to suggest he come to her house? It was after nine o'clock. She'd left Lenora's sister sitting at her bedside, and had been so grateful simply to be home. She'd kicked off her shoes, made a cup of coffee and reached for the TV remote control. She'd wanted to watch something mindless, something that might make her laugh. But before she'd hit the power button, her cell phone, still in her purse, had rung.

"Just wondered how your day went," Bruce had said, but she heard exhaustion and discouragement in his voice. "Are you still at the hospital? I might stop by."

"No, I've gone home." Before she knew it, she heard herself saying, "If you need to talk, you'd be welcome to come by."

Now, butterflies fluttering in her stomach, she was waiting for her doorbell to ring. She hardly knew him. They hadn't even dated! She never invited men she knew only casually into her home. This was her space, her sanctuary. She'd always believed she could tell as much about a person from seeing the inside of his home as she could if he stripped naked in front of her and babbled his deepest secrets. Every item she chose and how she displayed it, the colors she loved, her appreciation for clutter or simplicity, all spoke of how she saw herself, how she felt about herself. Letting him in the front door was like exposing herself.

The doorbell rang and she jerked. She was being absurd. He wouldn't notice her décor; men didn't. And anyway…she wasn't ashamed of her home or anything it said about her. Having a guy over for a cup of coffee was hardly an act of intimacy.

She opened her door to find he looked as worn as he'd sounded. Alarm squeezed her at the sight of this man, who ordinarily exuded such confidence, wearing discouragement as if it were a cologne.

"What happened?" she asked before she could stop herself. "You didn't find…?"

"Find…? No." He grimaced. "Neither hide nor hair."

She stood back. "Come in. Let me take your jacket." As he shrugged out of it and handed it to her, she was jarred by the sight of his shoulder holster and weapon. The leather straps somehow made his broad shoulders appear even more imposing. "Would you like a cup of coffee?" Her eyes narrowed. "Or have you eaten?"

"Surprisingly…yeah. I wanted to think. I stopped for a burger earlier."

She shook her head in disapproval.

"Coffee would be good."

Karin already had it brewing. She poured him a cup and freshened hers, added sugar and cream per their tastes and led the way back to the living room. Bruce sprawled at one end of her comfortable sofa, while Karin sat more sedately in a buttery-soft leather chair across from him.

"So what happened?" she asked.

"First, how's Lenora?"

"Actually, the doctor was encouraged today. She's getting restless. Jerking, some reflex responses to touch. She even had some facial twitches. I kept imagining she was about to open her mouth and say something." Karin gave a small shudder.

Anna and Enrico. Are they safe? That was what she'd imagined Lenora would ask first. How Karin dreaded answering that question.

"We got momentarily excited today when a patrol unit spotted a car matching the description of Escobar's. It had stolen plates." He grimaced. "When we closed in, we discovered it belonged to a group of runaway teens. They weren't real thrilled to see us."

"Do you think he's still around here?"

He frowned. "Yeah. Yeah, I do. I've been in touch with the FBI in case Escobar has crossed state lines with the kids. Neither they nor any other jurisdiction has picked up even a whisper. Besides, I checked with the hospital this morning. They've had a number of calls about Lenora's status. I'm wondering if he's one of the people calling."

Her eyes widened and her fingers tightened on her mug. "Do you mean... Is she in danger?"

"Probably not now, security is pretty tight in the ICU, but we'll need to be cautious if—when—she walks out of there. He's not going to like that." Bruce shook his head, then rubbed his neck as if it ached. "Unless he has delusions that she'll be sorry about what she did to him and is now longing for him. God knows."

Karin studied the man slouched so low on her sofa it might take a forklift to shift him off it. The lines carving his face were surely deeper than they'd been yesterday. With the stubble on his jaw, his dark hair disheveled, the gun nestled where he could grab it between one heartbeat and the next, he should have appeared dangerous. Instead, she read despondency in his posture, would have sworn she saw something wounded in his eyes. Was it just the frustration? Did he hate being thwarted that much?

"Your partner," she probed. "She's okay? And her sister's baby?"

"Huh?" He lifted his gaze from the mug to her. "Oh. Yeah. Kid's got a set of lungs, according to Molly."

Her mouth curved. "Babies come equipped that way, or so I'm told."

"Yeah, and think how long it takes to potty train 'em. Puppy learns in a week or two."

"And you don't have to send it to college, either."

At last he grinned, his body relaxing slightly.

"What I was *trying* to find out," she said with some exasperation, "is why you look like your puppy just got run over."

His grin, though genuine, had vanished as quickly as it appeared, gone in the blink of an eye. Now he tried to smile, but this effort was an abysmal failure. "That obvious, huh?"

"Mmm, hmm."

"It's this kid I've been spending time with. I signed up to be a Big Brother about a year ago—maybe a little longer now. I spend at least a few hours with Trevor pretty much every week."

She nodded to encourage him to keep talking.

"Trevor is twelve now. He's a great kid. Smart, funny. Life just keeps hitting on him." Bruce's voice was bleak. "He's small for his age, for starters. He has his own personal bully at his bus stop. His dad beat the crap out of his mother, who finally kicked him out two years back. Trev hasn't seen his dad since, although he calls sometimes. His mother tries, but she can barely hang on to a job for a couple of months at a time. I think she's on crack now. She's gone for a couple of days at a time pretty regularly, from what Trev says. But from the sound of it, she's been hurting lately, maybe suffering withdrawal, and she disappeared five or six days ago. She's never been gone that long before. He's scared."

"I should think!" she exclaimed.

"He called me. I called CPS. They sent a caseworker

and took him off to a receiving home." Now the agony was exposed, seeping. His expression suggested pure misery. "Trevor feels betrayed. Turns out he thought I'd take him home with me. And damn it, part of me wanted to. But with my hours, how can I? I might as well leave him completely on his own."

On impulse, she set down her coffee and circled the coffee table to sit beside him, instead, reaching out to grip his hand. He grabbed and held on as if to a lifeline. His face looked even more ravaged close up. However matter-of-fact his description of Trevor's situation and their relationship, he loved this boy, she thought.

"Do you still believe you did the right thing?" she asked. "Even after second-guessing yourself?"

"A couple hundred times?" His mouth twisted. "Yeah. I think so. But when I called, I was picturing him getting sent to a foster home. You know, mom, dad, maybe another kid. Instead he's being thrown into a dormitory-type situation with a bunch of bigger, tougher, meaner boys."

"Can't you find his mother?"

"So far, no cigar. She's probably semicomatose in a crack house somewhere." His shoulders moved in an unhappy shrug. "She may take weeks or months to surface if she's too far gone, and when she does, it may be in the morgue. Crap!" he said explosively. "She's all he has. And, damn it, she's tried!"

"Crack is supposed to be one of the worst addictions."

"Yeah, and I'm guessing she just lost her battle with it. But what's going to happen to Trev now?" He didn't expect a response, she could tell; he knew the answer. "I can't see a happy ending."

She bit her lip before saying tentatively, "Have you considered, if his mother can't be found…?"

His blank stare told her he hadn't.

"Taking him in? I mean, long term?" she suggested.

His grunt held incredulity. "Are you kidding? After the way I grew up? I have no more idea how to be a parent than his father did. Probably less. Parenting 101 in my house—kid gives you lip you backhand him. He breaks curfew? You pull out the leather belt. I have no idea what the responsible alternatives are. No. It's not happening." Subject closed.

Karin wanted to argue. She had never seen him interact with a child, never mind a defiant preadolescent, but she *had* seen him talk to a roomful of wary, wounded women with respect, compassion and blunt honesty that had allowed them to lower their guard. She didn't believe for a minute that Bruce Walker was a man who would ever backhand a child, much less become enraged enough to strike him with a leather belt.

Oh, God. Did he have scars?

That flash of speculation was enough to make her suddenly, exquisitely conscious of his body. Or perhaps of hers. No, the truth was, she'd been conscious of his from the moment she'd opened her door to him. She'd just…tamped down that awareness. She knew her cheeks were flushing, because heat seemed to rush through her veins. She was flushing all over.

Say something. Don't let him notice.

"Have you ever been angry at him?" she asked, almost at random.

"Trevor?" His eyebrows rose. "Mildly irritated."

"Then what makes you think…?"

"As parents, don't we all revert to what we learned at home?"

"We may have that tendency, but we can overcome it. The people who do revert are the ones who aren't self-aware. They just go with instinct. But lots of people who were abused as children turn into fine parents."

There, she congratulated herself. She sounded like the levelheaded therapist she was.

Yes, but she was still holding hands with Bruce. He didn't seem to want to let hers go, and she certainly hadn't made any effort to tug her hand free. Should she? Probably, but…

She sucked in a breath. His thumb had begun to move, making idle circles. She gave a tiny shiver of reaction.

"Thanks," he said huskily.

"For?" Her voice emerged barely above a whisper.

"Seeing hope." He paused, his gaze lingering on her face. His eyes had darkened to near charcoal. "Listening to me."

"It's…the least I could do."

"If you didn't want me to kiss you, it might have been smart if you'd stayed over there." Bruce jerked his head toward the chair.

She swallowed. "I think I must want you to kiss me."

"Good." The gravel in his voice was more pronounced. "Because I need you."

He tugged, and she went unresisting, unable to tear her eyes from his face. From his mouth, hard and yet somehow unbearably sensual.

A kiss. Just a kiss, Karin thought in near panic as his arm closed around her.

But she knew a lie when she told herself one.

CHAPTER SIX

SHE TASTED BETTER than any woman he'd ever kissed. From the minute she'd moved to the couch and taken his hand in hers, he'd thought, *I've got to kiss her. Soon.* And then, *Now.*

The urgency was gut level, stunning him. One minute he was tugging her toward him, the next he was devouring her mouth. The pillow of her lips, the warm dark cavern of her mouth, the slippery, sensuous slide of her tongue on his, ripped away any brain power.

Bruce yanked her on top of him, one hand tangled in the hair on the back of her head, the other rhythmically squeezing her buttock. That quick, he was rock hard against her. He tore his mouth from hers long enough to graze his teeth down her throat and lick the hollow at the base, salty and silky, then groaned and recaptured her lips.

She squirmed, and for a split second pure panic rocked him. She was going to pull away. God. He didn't know if he could bear to let her go.

But all she did was wriggle into a more comfortable position straddling him. The sensation of her thighs squeezing his hips was like a sonic boom, muffling the inner voice that counseled him to slow down. He *couldn't* go slow.

Bruce wrenched her shirt up and fumbled for the catch of her bra, even as she ended the kiss long enough to yank her own shirt over her head. He had a glimpse of her face: lips swollen and damp, hair wild, cheek whisker-burned, eyes riveted to his. And then he lowered his gaze to her breasts, more than a handful, peaked with tight, pink nipples.

He gripped her hips and lifted her so that he could take each breast in turn into his mouth, licking, suckling, tugging. Her back arched and her breath whistled out.

Hunger so primitive it was wordless claimed him. All he knew was that he needed to penetrate her. He had to *claim* her.

He pushed them both sideways, so she sprawled beneath him the length of the sofa. He reared to his knees to pull her pants and panties down with no ceremony. Her legs were gorgeous, long, taut and already wrapping around him. Sleek white belly and— yes!—dark blond curls at the apex of her thighs.

She half sat, and unbuttoned and unzipped his pants. Drawing them down, she gasped, "Do you have a condom?"

He was so crazed he didn't understand for a moment. When he did, he reached for his wallet in his back pocket. Did he have a condom? *Yes.* What would he have done if he hadn't…?

Moving had reminded him that he still wore both a shirt and his shoulder holster. Damn, damn, damn. From long practice he unbuckled the holster and dropped it over the arm of the sofa, yanked the shirt off and lifted himself from her long enough to free himself from the slacks, too.

Condom. He put it on himself with hands that shook, then bent to suckle her breast again. Finally, he kissed her deep and long, even as he found her opening and rammed in with no more finesse than a teenager his first time.

She was slick and tight and he couldn't go slow. He retreated and thrust again, and again, hard and fast. Her fingernails bit into his back and she nipped his neck sharply. Her hips bucked, and he fell with her from the sofa, crashing together onto their sides, never slowing. At one point she rose above him, before he flipped them again, banging against the coffee table, and climaxing as he pounded into her. She was spasming, too, and keening as he groaned.

As the wave washed out again, he collapsed. *The little death.* Yes, he simply could not move, could not form a conscious thought, could only feel satiated and boneless and deeply satisfied.

Awareness returned in micro increments. Pain on his upper arm. From where he hit the table. Or was it the floor? Rough-textured carpet beneath his knee, planted between her legs. His mouth sticking to her neck. *Drool?* That unwelcome realization produced a groan from the depths of his chest, and he rose onto his elbows.

"I'm flattening you."

"Hmm?" She looked, if it was possible, more stunned

than he felt. Maybe it wasn't postcoital bliss; maybe she was suffering from oxygen deprivation. He was a big man.

No place to roll. The coffee table, entirely too solid, blocked them on one side, the sofa on the other. Mumbling, he lifted himself awkwardly from her, then held out a hand.

Karin stared at it, as if unable to decipher the gesture. Then she whispered, "Oh." The next "Oh" emerged as a squeak, and she scrambled backward and to her feet. "Let me get…um…" She fled toward a short hall. A door closed behind her. Would she be coming back out?

Clothes. Bruce glanced around. In her absence, he got dressed, wincing every time he moved his right arm. Looked like a nice bruise was forming there.

As if a flashbulb were exploding in front of his eyes, he kept getting pictures. Ripping her clothes off like some kind of animal. Slamming into her. The crash to the floor. Squeezing her breasts. God. Had he left bruises on *her?*

What in the hell, he wondered, appalled, had happened to him? Should he leave before she reappeared? *If* she reappeared?

No. That would be unforgivable. *Slam, bam, thank you, ma'am.*

No.

With hands that felt clumsy, he picked up her clothing and carefully folded it, making a small pile on the coffee table. He slid the table back so it sat square to the sofa, restored to their places the pillows that had gone flying, then went to get a sponge from the kitchen to mop up the coffee spilled on the table. He was carrying the two mugs back to the kitchen when Karin returned down the hall, wearing sweats. Her hair, he saw with a lightning-quick assessment, was pulled back repressively. Even painfully. She didn't quite meet his eyes.

Without a word, he set the mugs in the sink and faced her. She hovered in the kitchen doorway, arms tightly crossed, her teeth on her lower lip.

After a minute, Bruce said, "I don't know where that came from."

She gave a peculiar laugh. "Me neither."

"I can be gentle. Even patient."

Voice as tightly strung as her body language, she said, "I didn't seem to have any problem with your technique."

At her words, he felt a jolt in his groin. No. She'd given as good as she got, and he hadn't mistaken the seemingly endless way her body had spasmed around his.

So. They'd had raw, even brutal, sex, and now they were both embarrassed. He grunted. *Embarrassed* didn't half cover it. He was shaken to know what he was capable of. What if she'd said *stop!* just before he'd penetrated her? *Could* he have stopped? He didn't know, and hated the not knowing. What separated him, then, from the monsters who had raped those women he'd met at A Woman's Hand?

"I hope, ah, that you don't have any bruises."

Alarm leaped into her eyes. "Especially visible ones."

"Yeah, not so good in your line of work." He braced

his hands on either side of the countertop and couldn't suppress a small wince.

"You're hurt," she said.

"Banged my shoulder."

Her teeth worried her lip again. "Oh."

He cleared his throat. "It was…amazing."

Color, already high in her cheeks, rose. "I've never done anything like that."

"Me neither." But, God help him, he wanted to do it again. Soon. With her. Bruce decided not to tell her that. Next time, he swore, he'd be so damn gentle, so considerate, she'd have to beg him to let go.

Assuming there was a next time.

"Can we have dinner tomorrow night?" he asked. "If something doesn't intervene?"

He was a homicide cop; "something" frequently did intervene.

He saw the hesitation—leading up to refusal—on her face. Oh, yeah, he'd panicked her.

"Just dinner," he coaxed. "If we can have wild sex, surely we can talk over the dinner table."

A parade of emotions crossed her face. No, not a parade, more like the Kentucky Derby, every emotion jostling for space, stretched out at a flat run. He'd have really liked to get a good look at each if only they'd slow down.

Finally, she sighed and dipped her head. "Yes. You're right. Dinner. Say, six?"

He agreed. She walked him to the door, offering no suggestion that he hang around, have a refill of that cup of coffee that had ended up spilled or—especially—spend the night. There, they eyed each other for a minute, their precise relationship uncomfortably ill defined. Thinking *What the hell,* Bruce stepped closer, tilted her chin up with one finger and kissed her.

He kept it light, gentle and generally everything their lovemaking hadn't been. The contact was still enough to stir something in him. She could become addictive, he thought, disquieted. The one comfort was that her mouth softened under his, and she appeared dazed when he lifted his head and, after clearing his throat, said, "Good night."

She'd backed inside and was locking up by the time he left the porch. Bruce got in to his car, started it, then sat there for a minute, trying to figure out whether this had been a really shitty day, or one of the best of his life.

TOO MANY OF KARIN'S new clients came to her looking just like this woman. Unlike many, this one had avoided a hospital stay. Her nose was plastered, however, after being broken, and the still-puffy flesh around both her eyes had progressed from being merely blackened to a rainbow of sickly colors.

Karin and she had already discussed her history with other men, and the escalating violence of this relationship.

"Tell me," Karin asked, "does Tyrone hurt you in bed, too?"

Destiny Malone gave her a grin that was startlingly wicked, appearing on that battered face. "You kidding, girl? 'Course he does! But in a good way, you know?"

Karin could count on one hand the times she'd blushed in a counseling session. She prayed the heat in her cheeks this time wasn't visible.

Oh, God, she thought in horror. *Did I ask because I needed to know for* her *sake? Or for mine?*

Had she been trying to figure out whether sex like she'd had with Bruce only happened if the man was violent by nature?

Maybe. But if the answer was yes and he was a brute—what did that say about *her* enthusiastic participation last night? Hadn't she actually *bitten* him? Karin cringed.

"He don't beat me or anything like that. It's just that he's hot for me. He say he can't get enough." Destiny smiled again, with some secret satisfaction. "And a woman, she's got to like that."

Yes. She did. Having a man desperate for her, rather than politely anticipating lovemaking, was an incredible aphrodisiac. Karin had had no idea.

"What if you say no?" she asked. "Does Tyrone accept that?"

Her carefully plucked brows rose in apparent surprise, momentarily widening her eyes. "'Course he does. You think I'd take him back if he *raped* me?"

"Ah… He does hit you," Karin reminded her.

"Yeah, but…but…" She scowled. "That's different."

"How?"

"Well, 'cuz…" She shifted in the seat, crossing her legs, uncrossing them, finally bursting out, "He only hits me when I been asking for it."

"Do you believe you *deserved* this beating?"

"I have this trouble, see." Shame suffused her gaze before she lowered it. "I like to shop."

Karin blinked.

Destiny, it developed, *really* liked to shop. She was pathologically driven to shop, and easily convinced herself that she needed that pair of shoes or that handbag or those jeans. She'd run up all her credit cards, then his. Sometimes she'd take things back, but mostly they went into her closet and often stayed there unworn. It was when she spent money they didn't have that Tyrone lost his temper.

So, okay. There were two problems to deal with: Tyrone's temper and Destiny's compulsive shopping. Karin was hugely relieved to feel herself shifting into professional mode. She'd had absolutely no business relating anything a client told her to herself. Particularly when that something was as intimate as whether she had bruises after sex.

As her day went on, she had trouble concentrating. She kept replaying last night's scene, from the moment she'd sat on the sofa next to him and taken his hand, to that last kiss on the doorstep. Remembering, Karin found herself getting aroused. She was both disconcerted and embarrassed. This wasn't like her! She'd always been the cool, calm, collected one, not so much a participant in life as an observer. She'd never really seen that as a negative; she *liked* maintaining a little distance.

Uh-huh. Forgot to do that last night, didn't you?

The awful thing was, Destiny Malone was right. A woman *did* have to like the feeling of being wanted so desperately. Karin shivered at the memory of his face, taut with urgency.

So, okay, maybe her previous experiences with sex had been a little *too* civilized. Maybe even tepid. Definitely lacking. But it gave her the creeps to think she'd been secretly craving that violent act.

Or…was it a man like Detective Bruce Walker she'd been craving? And what did *that* say about her?

Alone in her office at the end of the day, she squeezed her eyes shut and muttered, "Get a grip."

She just had time to make it home and change from a blazer and slacks to a more casual and comfortable pair of wide-legged pants and a V-necked, silk top before Bruce picked her up.

"News?" she asked before she even had the door all the way open. The question seemed to restore their relationship to a former place, when Lenora was the reason they were speaking at all.

She saw the answer on his face, but he shook his head anyway, lines furrowing his forehead.

"Molly is back, which is a help, but we won't be able to stay full-time on this. Upside is, the FBI is galvanized. Lots of good press if they find the kids, you know. The downside is, they're being their usual jackasses." His eyebrows rose. "Ready?"

Once they were in the car, he said, "Oh, I meant to ask you about the upcoming self-defense workshop. Are we going on with it?"

"I can't decide," she admitted. "I tend to think we should. If anything, what happened to Lenora highlights how much these women need the skills you're teaching."

"Canceling on them might send the message that, see, it's hopeless anyway," he agreed. "We don't want to do that."

They talked about the program a little more, including the question of whether another facility would be safer, but concluded that the moment when the women separated to go to cars was always the point of vulnerability.

"This time Molly will be with me, and we'll stick around until every woman's safely on her way."

Karin nodded, wondering about his partner. In the course of her work, she'd met her share of women cops, but still found them...a puzzle, was perhaps one way to put it. Her end of the business, the healing, was more traditionally feminine. She couldn't imagine stepping into the punitive role, or handling the physicality of it. The tendency was to believe that women who chose to go into law enforcement were mannish, but in her experience that wasn't at all true. They were gutsy; maybe, like the men, they enjoyed the adrenaline rush their work brought. But Karin had met many who were soft-spoken, pretty, feminine, even petite.

"What's Molly like?" she asked.

Bruce glanced from the road ahead at her. "Like?" he asked blankly, his tone one of typical masculine befuddlement.

"Young? Old? Married? Does she have kids?" She waved both hands. "You know."

"Oh. Um… Not old. Twenty-nine, and worrying about turning thirty. Unmarried—one of the reasons she's worried. She's always asking what's wrong with her."

"And you tell her…?" Karin probed.

"Nothing's wrong with her!" He shrugged in further bafflement. "She's always seeing some guy. She's the one who breaks it off."

"Hmm."

He shot her a grin. "Was that a therapist's 'hmm'? Or a mild expression of interest?"

Until now, the conversation had felt…strained. Maybe just in her imagination, but she didn't think so. She thought they'd both been pretending to hold a normal conversation. But all of a sudden her mood lightened. He didn't smile often, this cop, and maybe that was why each time he did she found herself newly fascinated. She loved the way his eyes crinkled, so that sometimes they, rather than his mouth, seemed to be doing the smiling.

She loosened up enough to laugh. "Habit, I'm afraid. Shake me if I start saying 'Tell me how you feel about that.'"

He grinned again, then said with satisfaction, and perhaps a little smugly, "A parking place! Damn, I'm good."

He had reason to be pleased; parking around the Pike Place Market was at a premium, and this spot was right in front of the open-air front. Artisans had their wares laid out on tables or blankets on the ground. Inside, under cover, shoppers could buy fresh-caught salmon or giant geoduck clams, local strawberries or armfuls of flowers.

Seattle's Pike Place Market was famous, having evolved from a simple farmer's market into a tourist draw that still offered the fresh produce, seafood and baked goods that local shoppers sought. Multiple levels of an idiosyncratic wooden structure descended from the foot of Pike Street down a steep bluff to the Puget Sound waterfront below. Several high-end restaurants occupied space in the market, along with art galleries, importers, boutiques and specialty shops of all kinds. The market had spread to blocks around, too, making it a shopping mecca, with kitchen, furniture and gift stores, wine merchants and more galleries.

"We're early," Bruce said. "Shall we wander?"

Releasing her seat belt and reaching eagerly for the door handle, Karin agreed. She couldn't remember the last time she'd come down here. It had been too long.

Doing something so *normal* with Bruce eased the discomfiture she felt even more. She wrinkled her nose at the sight of fish fillets spread over beds of ice but admired tables heaped with produce, some local, like the strawberries, some like ears of early corn trucked over the mountains in the early morning from the sunnier eastern side of the state. She hovered over a table of beautiful handcrafted jewelry, finally buying a pair of earrings. When she turned back around, Bruce handed her a bouquet he'd bought from a nearby flower vendor. Karin inhaled the scent of deep pink roses mixed with the simpler blooms of daisies and sprays of tiny flowers she thought were yarrow.

On impulse, she rose on her toes and kissed him lightly on the mouth. "Thank you. Nobody ever buys me flowers."

Eyes glinting, he said, "Maybe because it's coals to Newcastle. You grow enough."

"Cutting them myself isn't the same."

They had dinner at The Pink Door, a restaurant you almost had to be a local to find, and were lucky enough to be seated out on the trellis-enclosed deck as the sun was just setting. Inside, a trio played music that could have been performed in a Prohibition-era speakeasy. The rustic Italian menu used produce from the market.

Karin and Bruce sipped wine, ate at a leisurely pace, listened to music and talked with surprising ease about movies, books, politics and their jobs. Darkness descended, and tiny lights strung on the trellis lent fairy magic to the night. They were still engrossed in their conversation when the musicians finally put away their instruments and they could hear again the muffled sounds of city traffic.

She told Bruce about her childhood and coaxed stories from him about the tough neighborhood he'd grown up in and about his alienation from his own brothers, who had followed in their father's footsteps.

"Why were you different?" she asked.

Bruce began. "I don't know—" But he stopped. "No, that's not true. Me, I hung out at this community center. Some cops volunteered there. One of them became my idol." He shook his head, a wry smile on his mouth. "He was a great guy. He took me places, even to L.A. Lakers games. He had amazing seats. I couldn't believe how lucky I was. His wife was a really nice woman. I remember the first time I went to their house for dinner, she complained—I think he'd forgotten to pick something up at the store on the way home—and I shrank, waiting for him to wallop her."

He seemed momentarily lost in the past, and finally, Karin prodded, "What did he do?"

Bruce shook his head, his boyish astonishment still there. "He said I'm sorry and kissed her. She laughed and greeted me. The way she smiled at me, as if I was a real person, somebody she could hardly wait to get to know…" He cleared his throat. "I found out later that they couldn't have kids. They did finally adopt, a little girl from Colombia."

Some of the tables out on the deck were now empty, and couples at the others spoke quietly. The sound of a ferry horn was somehow haunting at night.

Very softly, so she didn't disrupt the mood, Karin asked, "Have you stayed in touch with them?"

"I haven't talked to them in a couple of years. I got an invitation to their daughter's wedding last summer and sent a present, but I couldn't get away. It would have been hard to go without…"

"Visiting your parents?"

He grunted agreement but didn't elaborate. After a surprisingly peaceful silence, Bruce stretched. "I suppose we should get going. We both have early mornings ahead."

Back in the car, they weren't three blocks from the Market before Karin realized she'd been kidding herself all night. All the talk about Mideast politics and art-house films hadn't in the slightest reduced her awareness of his body. Every movement, every flex of his muscles, had her remembering him unclothed. He reached for the gearshift, and she saw his big, capable hand cupping her breast or gripping her hip. She knew the taste of his skin, the timbre of his voice when he was aroused, the rasp of his sandpapery jaw. And she wanted him again.

He told a story about his days as a patrol officer in the Pioneer Square area; she asked a question or two. But it required a huge effort to sound...normal. A minute later, she could hardly remember what he'd said or why she had laughed politely.

He gave up talking, and in the next blocks she felt as if the air in the car had become thick, difficult to breathe.

A moment later, he pulled into her driveway. Turning off the engine, he said, "I'll walk you to your door."

Moment of truth. She wanted him to. She didn't want him to. She knew, of course, that he would kiss her, but not whether she'd risk asking him in.

They got out, Karin cradling the bouquet. The slam of the car doors was as startlingly loud as a gunshot in the sleeping neighborhood. The two walked in silence up to her porch, and Bruce waited while she unlocked and faced him.

After studying her face for a long moment, he smiled so ruefully she knew her panic must be blatant.

Voice a rumble, he asked, "Was the evening so bad?"

Karin laughed, if a little shakily. "No. Of course it wasn't. I had a wonderful time."

"But you haven't decided whether I'm man or beast."

Oh, dear. That was exactly it. Or...was it?

"I think," she admitted, "it's more that I'm wondering what *I* am."

His gaze was all too perceptive. "I see." He cleared his throat. "Here's my suggestion. We slow it down a bit. I kiss you good-night, then go home. Tomorrow I'll call you, and we'll talk about how our day is going, and maybe I'll call again late in the evening, just because I'm going to want to. And then we'll plan dinner again. Uh…if that works for you."

Filled with relief—because he wasn't pushing her? Or was it because he hadn't lost patience with her?— she nodded. "That works. Thank you."

He said something under his breath, which she couldn't quite make out, and then his lips found hers. He kissed her so softly a wondering breath was trapped in her throat. Their mouths brushed, pressed, nibbled. The moment was indescribably sweet. He sucked gently on her lower lip, and that breath escaped in a long sigh.

Bruce lifted his head and looked down at her. After a moment, he raised his hand, grazed his knuckle over her cheek, touched a fingertip to her mouth, then murmured, "Good night," and left her still standing stunned on her doorstep.

He was gone before she could whisper, "Stay."

CHAPTER SEVEN

BRUCE LAY IN BED and frowned at the ceiling. So, okay; he'd managed to kiss Karin gently and with finesse. The kiss had lasted maybe one minute, tops. If it had gone on for one more minute, that finesse would have been history. He'd had to make his escape before he lost control. He wanted her with a clawing need different from anything he'd ever felt before, a need that still had him aroused an hour later.

She got under his skin. If he could lose every remnant of control the way he did when they made love, what would happen if he lost his temper with her?

Unfortunately, he knew. He'd grown up seeing what he could become. With the combination of genes and environment, what he *would* become.

They'd had some great sex. If he had any sense at all, he would be satisfied with that and start running the other way, not woo her with dates. He'd decided long ago he wasn't husband and father material, not unless he wanted to follow in his father's footsteps. And, God—did he *want* to live day in and day out with this edgy feeling of obsession? He didn't like that she was in the back of his mind all the time, that he constantly wondered what she was doing, what she'd think about this, what she'd say about that. And this restless, prickling, violent need for her—that would drive him insane.

Do not walk. Run.

But even before he fell asleep, he knew he wouldn't. Couldn't.

SINCE TREVOR HAD BEEN so uncommunicative, on Friday Bruce called the social worker for an update. He sat in the squad room, his feet on the desk, chair leaning back precariously. Molly was late, having announced her intention to stop at Caffe Ladro for decent coffee on the way in. Bruce had given her his order.

"I just spoke with Trevor's father," Ms. Connelly told him. "Mr. DeShon is back in the Seattle area and eager to have his son. So that's good news."

Anger knifed him, and his chair squealed as he sat upright, his feet hitting the floor. Good news? What the hell was she doing in this job if she was really that naive? Or was she just glad to get one kid out of her hair?

Unclenching his jaw, Bruce said, "You are aware that Trevor's mother had to get a restraining order to keep Mr. DeShon from terrorizing her and Trevor?"

After a small hesitation, the social worker said, "I was informed there'd been allegations of abuse."

"Allegations?" Bruce didn't even try to keep the incredulity out of his voice. "How about multiple hospital visits."

"But I understand that Mr. DeShon never abused his son."

"Because MaryBeth sent Trevor to hide in his bedroom when his dad came home drunk and in a rage. She offered herself as a target to keep her kid safe."

"Mr. DeShon freely admits that he had an alcohol problem, but he has completed a treatment program and attends AA meetings twice a week. According to him— and he says his mentor in AA will confirm—he has been sober for two years now. He also completed an anger-management class. I believe that he was devastated to lose his family, particularly his son. Everyone deserves a second chance."

"Leopards don't change their spots," Bruce said flatly. "Once an abuser, always an abuser."

"According to police reports and his own story, he was always drunk when he hit his wife. If he stays sober…"

He snorted. "What are the chances of that?"

Her voice chilled. "Trevor deserves to have one of his parents. Clearly, that won't be his mother. And frankly, given his age I don't envision a better alternative for him. Do you?"

After a silent litany of swearing, he forced himself to admit she was right. What *was* the alternative? There weren't enough caring foster parents. Odds were high Trev would end up with the other kind, the ones who took kids in for the money paid by the state or who abused the kids in turn. Wade DeShon *had* worked at maintaining contact with his son. If the alleged two years' sobriety wasn't a scam, he deserved some real credit for it.

"Unfortunately, no."

"It's really important that you encourage Trevor to give his father a chance."

That stung. Was he supposed to lie to the boy? But again—he knew what she was getting at, and she was right.

"Okay," Bruce conceded. "But I'll be watching like a hawk. If DeShon screws up once, he's not getting another chance."

"People do make mistakes."

"He's made his. He's used up any possible excuses."

She wasn't thrilled with him by the end of the call, but he didn't care. His gut was churning. Wade DeShon was getting his kid back, and MaryBeth wouldn't be there to stand between them.

Trevor didn't know yet, and Ms. Connelly had warned Bruce off. She wanted to talk to him first herself. He had to respect her insistence.

Instead of hitting the road, Bruce spent most of the day on the phone and the Internet. He was becoming more convinced that Roberto Escobar had left the area. Bruce had laid out a map and calculated distances and routes. If Escobar was smart—and his successful disappearance with the kids suggested he was—he'd make sure he went somewhere he could blend in. In other words, someplace with a substantial Hispanic population. Yakima and Walla Walla qualified, but he'd know that Lenora's sister and husband followed the harvests in eastern Washington. He'd probably have met their friends and the husband's extended family. Roberto would want to avoid them.

Bruce's finger moved down the map, touching on one town after another in Oregon, then on into California. Escobar could vanish in Southern California, but getting there was the problem. Would the car make it? Traveling with two young children and no woman, he might be conspicuous. Where would they sleep and shop and eat on the way?

Bruce made phone calls to every jurisdiction he could think of, extracting promises to check the records of cheap motels, talk to gas station attendants, watch for that blue Buick. When he got hoarse, he turned to e-mail, sending photos and Escobar's license-plate number.

Then he repeated many of the same phone calls he'd made the other day in the hope of locating MaryBeth DeShon. No go. He couldn't believe she'd left the area. No, she wouldn't consciously abandon her son. It could be that her body just hadn't been found yet, or she hadn't been identified. Bruce was still betting on option three, the drug-induced stupor.

Goddamn it, MaryBeth, he thought, *Trevor* needs *you. Where are you?*

He called Karin midafternoon and had a brief, unsatisfactory conversation with her. No news on my end, he told her. No news on hers. She had only five minutes between clients, and he sensed her distraction. The call was…awkward.

It all added up to a worthless day.

Walking out to their cars at the end, Molly asked, "Is this one getting to you?"

He almost said, *Yeah, she's getting to me,* when he

realized his partner was asking about the case, not Karin. She had no idea he was dating anyone special right now, far less someone intimately involved in the current investigation.

"Ah...I guess so," he admitted. "You know I never like these domestic ones."

She slanted a knowing glance at him. "You seem worse than usual."

"I took it personally."

Her shrug eloquently conveyed her skepticism. *Maybe, but I don't believe that's the whole story.*

He hadn't told her about his talk with the social worker. Now he did, successfully distracting her. She'd hung out with him and Trev a couple of times. Like him, she had trouble believing a slug like DeShon was capable of living up to good intentions, however sincere.

Karin had been evasive when he'd asked if she was busy tonight. He wasn't enthusiastic about the idea of more fast food and an empty house, and stopping by the hospital ostensibly to check up on Lenora would smack of stalking. He phoned the receiving home and got permission, instead, to take Trevor out for pizza and a movie.

A group of boys watched TV in the living room, and the woman who let him in seemed okay. She yelled for Trevor, and when he didn't appear went upstairs to get him. Bruce had the distinct impression she'd had to drag the kid downstairs by his scruff.

"Have a good time," she said, enough sympathy in her voice that he figured Trevor had gotten lucky with this placement.

On the way out to the car, he asked, "You talk to Ms. Connelly?"

The boy gave him a look seething with misery and fear. "She said I have to live with my dad! Mom didn't even like him *calling*."

Bruce unlocked his car. "That's true. But he's made a lot of effort so he'd get a chance to see you again."

"You sound like *her*," Trevor said with loathing, and flung himself into the car.

Well. They were off to a good start.

Buckling himself in, Bruce asked, "When's he coming to get you?"

"Tomorrow!" Anguish filled his big brown eyes. "Can't I please stay with you, instead? I'm okay alone! You know I am!"

Hating himself, Bruce shook his head. "I told you why it wouldn't work. Besides, I don't think they'd let me take you now. Parents have first rights. Unless your dad screws up, Ms. Connelly won't consider other options."

"You mean, if he hits me."

Yeah. That was what he meant.

"Or," Bruce added, "doesn't live up to his job as a parent in other ways."

The boy's forehead wrinkled. "Like?"

"He doesn't come home when he promises you he will. Gets drunk a lot. Doesn't make sure you eat right or do your homework."

Trevor hunched and didn't say anything. They were both painfully aware that Bruce could be talking about MaryBeth as much as Wade.

"Pizza?" Bruce asked, starting the car.

Trevor's shoulders jerked.

Pizza it was.

Bruce tried talking to him some more while they ate, suggesting that living with his dad might not be all bad.

"I'm told he has a good job now," he said. "He might have a nice place."

Trevor gave him a look that said more clearly than words that he didn't care. Bruce suspected that indifference wouldn't survive if Dad turned out to own a big-screen TV and a Nintendo. An iPod for Christmas would go a long way toward softening any thirteen-year-old's heart. And Trev would be thirteen by then, officially a teenager.

"Hey, at least you'll be going to a new school. No Jackson at your bus stop."

Trevor's expression lightened. Bruce didn't mention that there were bullies everywhere.

They saw an idiotic action-adventure film that would have bored Bruce into somnolence if he hadn't seen how engaged Trevor was. His mom hadn't often had the money for movies. Bruce had taken Trevor a few times, but had preferred spending their time together playing sports, going places like the science center or talking.

On the drive back to the receiving home, Trevor chattered at first about the movie, only falling silent as they got close. When Bruce pulled up to the curb, the boy turned to him and spoke fast. "Please. Please ask if I can come live with you. You're a cop and everything! I bet they'd say yes." He swallowed. He finished with one soft, hopeless "Please."

God. Bruce's hands flexed on the steering wheel. "I'm sorry."

With a strangled sob, Trevor fumbled for the seat-belt fastening and then the door handle. He flew up the driveway without waiting for Bruce, flung open the door and disappeared inside. Bruce followed more slowly, exchanged a few words with the foster mom, then left.

He got back in to his car and sat there for a long time, feeling like a low form of life. He wanted to believe that it meant something to Trev that he'd come tonight, spent time with him, listened to his unhappiness, but he couldn't believe it. All he'd done was once again let down a boy who'd known a lifetime of letdowns.

Jaw flexed, he thought, By God, if Wade DeShon so much as raised a hand toward Trev...

You'll what? Ride to the rescue? Just like you did this time? his inner voice mocked. *Face it. You can't be trusted any more than his father can.*

Knowing he'd done the right thing was cold comfort.

ON FRIDAY Karin realized that Lenora's coma was becoming noticeably lighter; her hands or legs jerked more, her eyelids fluttered frequently and occasionally she moaned or murmured. A couple of days ago, Karin was still talking as much to herself as to the unresponsive woman in the bed. She would unwind from her day by telling stories from her childhood or recounting snippets she'd read in the newspaper. Now...now she hung on every twitch, felt her anxiety ratchet at every mumble. Were Lenora's eyes about to open? Would *she* be in there? Or only some damaged semblance of herself?

The possibilities covered a wide spectrum. She might never regain consciousness at all. She might begin to have seizures and worsen. She might open her eyes but be severely brain damaged. The likelihood was that she'd have suffered at least some brain damage.

Or she might open her eyes, look around with panic and disorientation and then remember.

Lenora was both praying for and dreading the last possibility.

She gave up at last and went home to her empty house. She never used to think of her house that way. She'd always been glad to be home, comforted by the surroundings she'd created, anticipating the hour she meant to spend in her garden the next morning. Now the emptiness was the first thing that hit her when she walked in the front door. How had that happened?

She knew, but didn't want to think about it.

Her voice-mail box was as empty as the house. She felt a little lurch of disappointment. Hadn't Bruce said he'd call at the end of the day "just because he'd want to"? Had he called and not bothered to leave a message? Or had he been busy and not even thought about her this evening?

Which would she prefer to be the truth?

Karin kept listening for the phone even as she brushed her teeth and got ready for bed, but it never rang. She was dismayed to realize how much she wanted to hear his voice.

He finally did call at lunchtime the next day, other voices audible in the background. She was working her one Saturday a month. "Dinner tonight?"

"Sure." She hesitated, then said, "Why don't I cook."

Moment of silence. "Are you sure you want to after a long day?"

"I made a vegetarian chili last weekend and froze it. I'll warm it up, make a salad, some corn bread…"

"Sold."

They agreed on a time, exchanged a few "no news" remarks and said goodbye. Karin set down the phone, aware of her uneven heartbeat and the flush that seemed to be spreading from her chest out. She knew the cause: it was the way his voice had deepened and become more resonant when she suggested they eat at her place. He thought the invitation meant more than a simple meal. And maybe, Karin admitted to herself, it did. She'd offered on impulse, but knew perfectly well that impulses had roots that plunged deep. She wouldn't have invited him into her home again if she hadn't wanted him here, with all that encompassed.

Karin loved her job, but this was the rare day when she'd had to force herself to listen carefully and give her best. A part of her had pulled away and was giddy with anticipation, like a teenager daydreaming in class.

At home, she had time to change into jeans and a T-shirt and get the corn bread in the oven before she heard the doorbell.

Bruce looked as good as he always did to her. Not just sexy and a little dangerous, but also *solid*. Some of that was physical—he was big and strongly built, and she'd known from the first time she saw him that he would defend not just her but anyone he deemed vulnerable, with his life if necessary. But she knew just as surely that he could be depended on. He wasn't a man who'd ever let anyone down if he could help it.

In the end, that quality meant more than broad shoulders or a smile that jolted her heart.

Like the one he was giving her now. He was drinking in the sight of her face as if he'd been hungering for it. Once again, she could tell he was tired, but his smile changed the deep-carved lines, lessening the weariness and depression she sensed.

"Hey," she said, and rose on tiptoe to meet his quick, hard kiss as if her response was a given. And wasn't it? They'd become lovers, after all, however queasy she still was about that first time.

She hung up his coat and he followed her to the kitchen, where she refused his offer to help, then changed her mind to the extent of letting him uncork the wine and pour them both glasses. He watched her start the chili heating, then begin chopping vegetables for the salad.

They talked about Lenora, and he told her about some of the leads he'd pursued. After newspaper coverage, both the Seattle PD and the FBI had been inundated with tips, none of which had panned out. He'd located another of Roberto's supposed friends, only to be received with surprise.

"Says he hasn't seen Escobar in a year or more," Bruce said.

"And you believed him?"

"Yeah, I do. I had the feeling he hardly remembered the guy." He rubbed a hand over his face. "I was able to confirm that another guy on my list was deported a couple of months ago."

"Do you think…" She bit her lip, hating to articulate her worst fear.

"That they're dead?"

Karin nodded.

"No. If he'd intended to do it, he'd have killed the kids and himself that night. He'd have made it splashy." Bruce grimaced. "Sorry. Bad choice of words. But you get what I mean. He'd have wanted everyone to know. The more I learn about our Roberto, the more convinced I am that he believes he's completely justified in everything he's done. He's undoubtedly angry that his life has been inconvenienced. With no remorse, he has no motive for suicide."

What he didn't say, but they both knew, was that Roberto might well have motive to kill the children.

Be good for your daddy, Karin thought, her heart clenched in fear for Anna and Enrico. *Very, very good.*

Carrying the salad to the table, she asked, "Have you talked to Trevor?"

The boy's name was enough to change Bruce's expression. Apparently his Little Brother was the source of the unhappiness she'd sensed.

He set the wine bottle on the table. "Yeah. God." Anger vibrated in his voice. "The DSHS worker contacted his father. They're convinced, since he completed an anger-management class and alcohol treatment, that he's ready to be a great dad. Never mind that Trevor's scared to death of him."

Karin hesitated, choosing her words with care. This conversation was important; dinner could wait. "You don't believe it's possible he's changed?"

"Do you?" he asked incredulously.

"I don't know him."

"You'd never met Escobar, either."

"But I knew him through his wife's eyes. Her view was more sympathetic than you'd expect. For a long time, she was an apologist. Everything was her fault. He had a right." She waggled her hands. "You know."

"Trevor's mother didn't think Wade had a right. She put up with his abuse as long as she did out of fear of being on her own with a kid. She'd have done anything to protect Trev from his father."

"My point, I guess, is that some people *can* change. There's a wide gulf between someone like Roberto, who is incapable of what we consider normal human emotions or empathy, and someone who lashes out in anger because of depression or despair. Alcohol abuse plays a big part in that. So yes, I do believe some people can change. Why would I be in the profession I am if I didn't?" She held up a hand when she saw his expression. "No, I'm not saying Trevor's father is one of those people. I *don't* know him. But if his dad is genuinely trying, is it possible that Trevor's better off with him than he would be in a foster home?"

Bruce scowled at her. "I can't decide if I like your

relentless determination to be fair-minded and logical, or whether I really hate it."

Her mouth curved. "You must like it, or you wouldn't be here."

"Maybe I'm here because I think you're sexy."

She gave him a saucy smile. "That's okay, too."

She fetched the pot of chili and the bread, and then they sat down. As they ate, Bruce talked some more about Trevor: his unhappiness, how much he must be worrying about his mother, his renewed pleas and obvious feeling of betrayal that Bruce couldn't take him in.

"I felt like scum last night after I dropped him off."

"You should have called me." She flushed. "I mean, unless you had someone else you could talk to."

His focus on her was absolute. "No. I just went home. It was pretty late."

Tilting her head, Karin observed, "You really love him, don't you?"

"Love?" His dark eyebrows rose. "That's a strong word. I don't know that I've 'loved' anyone since I was a kid and still bought into the idea that's how you should feel about your parents."

Karin could only gape. "How can you never have loved anyone? Haven't you been *in* love? What about your friends? Don't you call that love?"

His face, formerly expressive, had become impassive. "I hadn't thought of friendships quite that way, no. There've been women, but nobody that serious. I made up my mind by the time I was ten years old that I wouldn't ever marry. I never wanted to have the right to rule and terrorize and hurt the way my father believed he did."

Never marry? Karin struggled to hide her shock. Did that mean she would be a fool to fall in love with *him?* Or a worse fool if she already had?

Thank goodness her work as a therapist had given her plenty of experience in hiding dismay and, instead, asking reasoned questions.

"You've surely met people since who are in happy marriages, starting with the police officer who was your mentor."

"Yeah, I have. But I'm too much like my father." He paused, turning the wineglass in his hand, his expression bleak. "I look like him. I could *be* him at this age."

"Who you are inside has nothing to do with how you look."

"His genes made me," he said flatly.

Karin shook her head. "No. They're part of you. But if he'd been raised differently, would he have been the same man? What about Enrico? Do you believe he's destined to be like his father, no matter how he grows up?"

She saw that he didn't.

"Or Trevor?" she continued, trying to sound merely persuasive and not desperate. How could he believe something so terrible about himself, discounting the day-to-day proof of what kind of man he really was? "You couldn't feel the way you do about him if you thought he was doomed to be a violent alcoholic."

"For both Trevor and Enrico, their mothers have had

a powerful influence. Mine was a victim. She never protected us kids. Far as she was concerned, he had a right."

Imagining the devastation of the boy he'd been almost broke Karin's heart. What was truly astonishing was how he *had* escaped his father's mold. The tragedy was that he'd done something so extraordinary, yet couldn't recognize he had.

"You are not your father," she repeated, having no idea what else she could say. How often would he have to hear it to believe it?

After a minute, his mouth twisted. "No. I know I'm not. I've spent a lifetime making damn sure I'm not. But I've also been careful to avoid putting myself in a spot where the instinct is to repeat what I heard."

"Parenting."

"Exactly."

"Trevor knows in his heart he can trust you. It's sad that you doubt what he can see so easily."

He just looked at her, and she could tell he wasn't really hearing.

"Hey," he said. "I promised the caseworker I'd pretend to Trevor that this was a great idea, and I did. Wade DeShon will out himself quickly enough if he's still the same drunken son of a bitch. When that happens, he'd damn well better not hurt Trevor."

When. Not if.

Karin found herself hoping quite passionately that Trevor's dad truly had changed. Maybe his redemption would have some impact on Bruce's pigheaded determination to believe the past shaped him.

But she, too, worried that Trevor might end up hurt. Her chest felt tight at the thought of so many children so much at the mercy of parents they ought to be able to trust. Every day, she saw both women and children wounded by someone who had promised to love them.

In her own way, she had as many doubts as Bruce did. She didn't know if she could ever trust in something so fragile, so often shattered. Thinking about the near violence with which Bruce had taken her was enough again to awaken disquiet. Did it mean he had something of his father in him, despite her attempts to persuade him otherwise?

Karin didn't believe it. *Couldn't* believe it. Yet the unease she'd felt about him reawakened.

Man or beast? Wasn't that how he'd posed the question?

Karin was struck by a terrifying realization. She was attracted to both sides of him. She wanted to make love with him again, whichever he was.

What does that say about me?

"Let me help clear the table," he said.

"No." Her voice came out oddly. "Let's not bother right now."

He went very still, his eyes darkening. "After what I said about never marrying, I thought you'd boot me out right after dinner."

"Where did you get the idea *I* want to get married?"

Karin heard herself in astonishment. She did want to love forever; she'd always believed, with all her heart, that someday she would marry, and her marriage would last forever. But however powerful the dream, right now it meant nothing compared with her need to have this man hold her again, become *part* of her again.

His chair rocked as he stood. She wasn't even aware of rising, and yet somehow she and he met at the foot of the table, and kissed as if they had both been starved for each other.

CHAPTER EIGHT

THE SECOND SELF-DEFENSE workshop had a very different tone from the first. Bruce and Molly arrived early and stood, deliberately conspicuous, in positions to intercept anyone entering the parking lot besides the participants. Still, the women all scurried into the clinic, their body language fearful.

Inside, heads bent together, and Karin heard the murmurs.

"Were you still here…?"

"Have they caught him?"

"Someone told me…"

After Karin thanked them all for coming and Bruce had introduced his partner, he had the sense to tell them briefly, gravely, about the assault and about the murder of Lenora's aunt and abduction of Enrico and Anna. He was honest about the lack of progress in finding Roberto, about Lenora's coma, about fears for the children. That honesty seemed to reassure the women in a way that platitudes wouldn't have. Heads nodded, backs straightened, and Karin sensed the renewed determination to learn what he had to teach.

Molly Beckstead might as well have been a college student as a woman who was almost thirty. Her eyes were bright blue, she had a snub nose and dark hair and she couldn't have weighed more than a hundred and fifteen pounds. After being introduced, she apologized for missing the previous week's session and told them about her new niece.

She was still talking when Bruce grabbed her from behind. In a flurry of movements so blindingly fast Karin couldn't separate them, she had him flat on his back, one arm bent at an excruciating angle.

"Pax," he said, and she laughed and let him up.

He climbed to his feet with an exaggerated groan that delighted the participants.

Much of this session was spent with the women paired up, earnestly trying out the releases Bruce and Molly demonstrated.

Watching the women gain confidence as they suc-ceeded in breaking even Bruce's grip filled Karin with triumph and a feeling of achievement. When Tonya, a shy eighteen-year-old who'd been raped, beaten and left for dead, swung around and planted a knee in Bruce's groin, then gasped and clapped her hand over her mouth as he crumpled to his knees, Karin stepped forward. But he mumbled something, Tonya giggled behind her hand, then beamed with shining satisfaction as the others laughed.

Instead of scurrying out the way they'd come, the women departed in a block, marching shoulder to shoulder as they escorted one another to their cars.

Perhaps being guarded by Molly and Bruce made them feel secure, but Karin suspected it was more: at least as a group, they felt courage they'd lost, and she actually had tears burn in her eyes as she watched them wordlessly work together to be sure they all got safely on their way home.

Afterward she went out with Bruce and Molly for coffee, and she had so much fun it was nearly midnight before she could tear herself away. She'd be tired tomorrow, but it was worth it. Molly, she thought, might become a friend, and Karin began to question all her reasons for not socializing with cops. With friends, she'd always preferred to escape the grim stories she heard all day, but laughing at a macabre yet also ludicrous tale Molly told of a man who was determined to rob a convenience store and died from sheer idiocy, it struck her how much she pretended with most people.

I'm a professional, she went out of her way to convey. *My days are like yours.* But her days *weren't* like a dentist's or a nurse's or a computer programmer's. They weren't like anyone else's she knew. Tonight, she'd felt herself relax in a way she usually couldn't. There was a freedom to being able to laugh without shame at a story that would have horrified most people.

Bruce gave her a quick kiss on the cheek when they parted at their cars. Karin saw Molly's startled and then speculative glance, and realized he hadn't told her he and Karin had a relationship. Weren't Molly and Bruce close enough friends to confide in each other? Or did he not consider it that important?

Karin rolled her eyes and fastened her seat belt. She was worse than a lovesick teenager, wondering whether he didn't really like her after all, or whether he was embarrassed to have it known he was dating her.

"You're a grown woman," she muttered, and turned the key in the ignition.

As the week went on, Karin talked to Bruce at least twice a day. They saw each other whenever they could, and it seemed impossible for her to get enough of him. She felt a cramp of longing at the very sight of him, and her body would soften and yearn in a way that should have embarrassed her but somehow didn't. As far as she could tell, he was as insatiable for her; whenever he spotted her, his gaze would find her face with a hungry intensity she understood.

It was scary to feel so much, to be so obsessed, about a man who'd told her bluntly that he'd never as an adult felt love for anyone and that he didn't intend ever to marry. Was what they had now all she could hope for? When she was with him, she thought it might be, but at night after he left and she'd gone to bed alone, she knew she was lying to herself. She wanted to be loved, and by a man as fully committed as she was. She wanted someone who would be beside her at night, across the breakfast table in the morning, not just ready to come when she needed him, but already *here,* part of every day.

With Monday night the exception, she did spend at least a little time every evening at Lenora's hospital bedside. Karin wasn't completely sure what drove her, but guilt was clearly part of the mix. She knew she wasn't really at fault. On one level, at least, she knew. If Roberto hadn't tracked his wife to the safe house—and how else had he found her that evening?—Cecilia was right when she said that the attack had been inevitable. At a different time and place, even more people might have been hurt. What if Cecilia had been walking right beside Lenora, for example?

But Karin finally understood why her patients were so slow to let go of unwarranted guilt. There were too many ways to blame yourself. *If I'd done that, thought of this, planned instead of proceeding thoughtlessly...* She could travel the twisted paths of second thoughts well into the night. Rationally, she was convinced that the assault wasn't her fault, but down deeper, she kept blaming herself.

And as Lenora became more restless day by day, Karin's incipient sense of doom deepened. She dreaded Lenora's waking, and dreaded the possibility that she wouldn't.

She tried talking to Jerlyn, one of the two remaining founders of the clinic. Now in her fifties, Jerlyn might have been an aging hippie, her dark hair graying and invariably worn in a braid wound atop her head, her feet shod in Birkenstocks or Earth Shoes, her skirts from India, the necklaces and long, dangling earrings she liked African or Indonesian. Jerlyn's gentle face hid a sharp mind and a heart filled with compassion.

What was disturbing was how little good the talk did Karin. She'd counseled too many women herself, and she recognized Jerlyn's strategies instantly, understood the tenor of her questions, knew what answers were expected. She found herself feeling sulky and then resistant. She wanted to say, *Can't you talk to me as a friend instead of a therapist?* To see how ingrained that style of relating to people was in a woman she'd viewed as a mentor stung a little. Did she do that to people, too? She remembered Bruce asking once whether her "hmm" was the counselor speaking or the woman, and winced.

Thursday, Bruce called to inform her that he and Molly had "caught" another homicide. The powers-that-be thought the trail was cold on the Escobar investigation. And after all, the FBI was working the abduction of the children, as well.

Her heart sank. "You won't give up?"

"No. I'm just going to have less time to work on finding him." In the background someone spoke to him, and he muffled the phone. A minute later, he was back. "Got to go. But don't worry. Every department from Blaine to San Diego is watching for them. Sooner or later, someone will spot him."

Would they? she questioned bleakly, ending the call. Roberto and the children had seemingly vanished. Bruce's attention wasn't the only one that would be waning. Crimes happened every day. All police departments must be flooded with notices asking them to be on the watch. Inevitably, the most recent notices would be at the forefront of their minds. How easy for a Hispanic man and two small children to pass unnoticed at a season when migrant workers were traveling the West Coast.

She wanted to have faith, but that, too, was waning.

"CAN I GET A HOT DOG, Dad?" Trevor asked.

Both men, one on each side of him, turned their heads, but at the crack of a bat striking the ball looked back toward the field. The baseball shot outside the line, foul, and the momentary excitement in the crowd at SafeCo Field settled back to an anticipatory hum.

It was a nice day, only a few cumulus clouds visible, and the retractable roof of the stadium was open. This was the first Mariners game Bruce had made it to this season, but it wasn't baseball that had drawn him today; the sport on the field could have been curling for all he cared. Damn it, he'd intended to spend his Saturday with Karin. But he couldn't say no to this chance to assess for himself Wade DeShon's fitness to have his son.

Bruce had to admit it was decent of Wade to suggest he join Trevor and him at the game. Or maybe it was just smart. Bruce had no idea what Trevor had said about him, but Wade must be able to guess that Bruce wouldn't be enthusiastic about this father-son reunion.

When he picked them up, he'd been startled by their resemblance, for a moment not sure what to feel. He'd come simmering with hostility, but it was hard to hate a man with Trevor's face.

Bruce had always thought of Trevor as taking after his mother, since they were both brown-haired and slight, but the kid's features and hazel eyes were unquestionably his dad's. His father wasn't a big man, Bruce noticed, but he must be five foot nine or ten, so there was hope for Trev.

The two men had shaken hands warily, feigning cordiality for the twelve-year-old's sake. Trevor was really excited, not seeming to notice the way Bruce assessed Wade, or the way his dad stiffened.

Fortunately, the game had been a good one, tied up in the seventh inning at two runs each.

Now, settling back in his seat, Wade said with mock dismay, "You're hungry already?"

"Yeah!" Trevor claimed.

"A hot dog sounds good," Bruce said. "I'll go out with him. Time to visit the john."

Wade reached for his wallet.

"I'll get it," Bruce said.

The other man's jaw tightened, but after a minute he gave a clipped nod.

"You want us to bring you something?" Bruce asked.

"Ah, hell, if everyone else is having a dog…"

He put in his drink order, too, and Bruce and Trevor stepped over legs to the aisle. Walking up the stairs, Bruce laid a hand on the boy's shoulder. "How's it going with your dad?" he asked.

They'd talked a couple of times on the phone, but Trevor had mostly mumbled, "He's okay."

Now he said again, "He's okay," but with more animation, as if he meant it. "He's being really nice. He told me how bad he feels about what a jerk he was. That's not the word he used, but he said I shouldn't say what he did."

Bruce suppressed a grin. "Probably a good idea."

They used the bathroom, then got in line at the concession stand. Bruce persuaded Trevor to talk about his new school, which he really liked.

The boy scrunched up his face, adding with more typical pessimism, "So far."

Bruce laughed this time, and they carried their tray of drinks and bag of hot dogs back to their seats.

Wade offered to repay him; Bruce declined, even though he was a little embarrassed by the whole thing. It was a pissing contest, he knew damn well. All afternoon, these two adult men had been silently warring over who knew best what Trevor liked or wanted, and who would pay for it. The kid remained oblivious, thank God.

The Mariners pulled one more run out of the hat and won. Trevor admitted to being sick to his stomach by the time they walked out of the stadium to the car.

During the drive home, it seemed as if the conversation was all Wade and Trevor. They talked about a movie they'd rented last night, about homework, about stuff Trevor could do this summer.

Bruce forced himself to put in a word now and again, but got quieter and quieter without either of the other two noticing. His chest felt tight, and he finally identified what was wrong.

He was jealous. Trevor didn't need him anymore.

Didn't *think* he needed him, Bruce corrected himself. Wade had yet to prove himself. Putting on a good front for a few days, a week, was easy. Whether he'd stay such a good guy once the novelty of parenting wore off was another matter. Trevor could be a butt; what kid wasn't sometimes? Would a man whose habit was to express his frustration with his fists be able to respond appropriately?

Bruce would believe it when he saw it.

Yeah, he thought. Trevor would still need him, even if he didn't know it yet.

"Good game," he agreed, letting them out in front of the small, white-frame house in Ballard that was now home to a boy who'd never lived in a real house before. He lightly cuffed Trevor on the shoulder and said, "Talk to you soon," then accepted Wade's hand for a shake.

Their eyes met and held. "You be good to him," Bruce said.

"Count on it," Trevor's father told him.

Real quiet, so the boy didn't hear, Bruce said, "I plan to make sure of it."

Damned if he didn't enjoy the flare of anger he saw on Wade's face, as if in provoking it, he himself had somehow won.

Trevor bounced impatiently on the sidewalk. "Come *on,* Dad!"

Eyes narrowed, Wade murmured, "Watch me," and got out.

Bruce did, as the two walked up to the front door, talking and laughing all the way. His fingers tightened on the steering wheel and his stomach roiled.

Shouldn't have eaten the hot dogs.

At last, he made himself put the car in gear.

Oh, yeah, he'd be watching.

TUESDAY MORNING, Susan put the call through to Karin when she was between patients. "A Yolanda Muñoz," she said.

Karin's heart skipped a beat. Lenora's sister had never phoned her at A Woman's Hand. Something had changed. She pushed the button for line one. "Yolanda?"

The woman's voice was charged with excitement. "Lenora—she's awake! Still confused, but she knows who I am!"

"What does the doctor say?"

"He thinks it's a miracle." She was clearly giddy. "The way they all shook their heads, I knew they thought she would die. But she's made them all wrong."

"Thank God," Karin whispered.

"Yes. I've prayed and prayed. He saved her, because Anna and Enrico need her."

Karin bit her lip so hard she tasted blood. "Have you told her…?"

After a long silence, Yolanda returned a subdued "She hasn't asked yet. It just happened. I left Imelda with her so I could call you."

Imelda was her oldest, a plump, sweet girl of fourteen.

More haltingly, Yolanda said, "I was hoping…I thought, if you were here…"

"I have one more client to see, then I'll leave. I should be there in an hour and a half."

"An hour and a half? That should be all right. The doctor wants to examine her. I won't let her ask until you're here."

Karin wanted with all her heart not to be there when Lenora found out that her husband had murdered her aunt and taken the children. But she wasn't quite coward enough to find an excuse. And it wasn't as if she didn't talk every day with distraught women about the most traumatic of subjects.

Still, this was different. She'd actually seen the attack. It had happened on her watch, so to speak. No matter how hard she'd tried, she hadn't quite convinced herself that she didn't share some blame.

Not sure if anyone else would think to call Bruce, as the investigating officer, immediately, she did.

"I only have a minute," she said when he answered his cell phone. "I just heard from Yolanda Muñoz. Lenora woke up."

"My God. Is she talking?"

"Uh…" Karin reviewed the conversation in her mind. "I don't know. Yolanda said she recognized her, and that the doctor was doing an exam. She said Lenora was still confused."

"Are you going over to the hospital?"

"At five."

"We'll want to interview her as soon as possible. I can't get away yet. Can you phone me once you've seen her?"

She promised she would, and then had Susan send her last client of the day in. Fortunately, Lila Wang didn't require great concentration. A pretty Asian woman who had been emotionally abused by a boyfriend, she was upbeat about a new job, and only slightly apprehensive about the move to San Francisco that it would entail. Karin was able to reassure her that she was ready. The time when Lila had needed her was past, to both their satisfaction, although Karin always felt a pang at this moment, as if she were a parent releasing a child to the world.

She walked Lila out and they hugged, Lila promising to phone once she was settled to let Karin know how she was doing.

The moment the woman was out the door, Karin snatched up her purse, gave a hurried explanation to Jerlyn, who'd emerged from her office, and rushed to her car.

Relatives crowded around Lenora's bed at the hospital. All were in a state of high emotion, exclaiming in Spanish over the top of one another and so fast that Karin, who did speak the language, could barely pick out a few words. On the edge of the crowd, Yolanda was wiping tears from her cheeks.

A nurse, who'd hurried in right in front of Karin, said firmly, "Please! Only two visitors at a time!"

Nobody paid her any attention. Yolanda did spot Karin, though, and her face lit with relief.

"*¡La médica està aqui!*" She flapped her hands and shooed the cluster of children and adults back from the bed, telling them to let Karin through.

Lenora lay against the pillows, face wan, distress seeming to ooze from her, and yet the return of life had changed her features to someone Karin was intensely grateful to recognize.

Tears burning the back of her eyes, she stepped to the edge of the bed and carefully took Lenora's hand. "I'm so glad to see you awake."

The dark eyes examined her, the bewilderment in them heartbreaking. For a moment Karin was certain she didn't recognize her, but at last her forehead crinkled and she murmured, a mere breath of air, "Karin?"

"Yes." Karin swallowed. "We've been so worried about you."

"I don't understand." Her gaze wandered to the nurse, and from face to face in the crowd of relatives Yolanda had herded to the foot of the bed.

"You were hit in the head." She hesitated. "Do you remember?"

Lenora shook her head.

Karin looked an appeal to Lenora's sister, who stayed back but said, "She wants to know where Roberto is."

Oh, Lord. She didn't even remember fleeing to the safe house?

Karin pressed her hand. "You left Roberto," she said bluntly. "You saved money for weeks so you'd have enough to get by for a while."

The dark eyes stared at her without comprehension. "Anna? Enrico?"

Karin drew a deep breath, and made a decision. "They're with Roberto."

"Oh." Something like relief relaxed her face. On some level, she had been anxious about their absence. But it seemed too soon to tell her that her husband was the one who had hurt her and had stolen her children.

"Why don't we let you rest," Karin murmured.

"Yes," she whispered, peering uncertainly again at the faces staring back at her, as if she didn't understand quite who they were or why they were there.

Her uncle was present, Karin saw, out of the corner of her eye, his face heavily lined with grief, but he'd had the sense not to say anything about his wife or Lenora's children. As much as Lenora *did* grasp, she would soon enough wonder about her aunt Julia's absence and why Roberto didn't bring the children to visit her. But tomorrow, Karin thought, was time enough to stun her with the awful events she'd missed.

"You're going to be fine," she said, smiling, her vision blurred with tears. "Don't worry, Lenora. Everything will come back to you. Don't hurry it."

A tiny nod, and it seemed to her that the small dark-haired woman allowed herself to relax. Her eyes drifted shut.

Yolanda turned and fiercely flapped her hands again. The rest of the family dutifully filed out, followed by her and Karin. The nurse remained, her hand on Lenora's wrist as she checked her pulse.

"You don't think we should have told her?" Yolanda demanded the minute they were out in the hall.

"Not yet. You're right. She's still confused. I think it would be better if we let her recover a little before we distress her."

Or had she just taken the coward's way out?

Yolanda looked no more convinced than Karin felt. "What do I say if she asks for the children?"

"I don't believe we should lie to her," Karin said slowly. "When she gets insistent, then we'll have to tell her. For now, you can just say again that they're with Roberto."

Lenora's sister nodded, grudging. "You'll come again, *sí?*"

"*Sí*. First thing in the morning, before I go to work."

"That policeman—he'll want to talk to her, won't he?"

"Yes, but not until Lenora remembers what happened." She hoped; having a police officer loom over her bed, asking questions, would certainly mean that Lenora would have to be offered a far more complete explanation than she'd seemed to want tonight.

"Will you call him? Tell him he would upset her?"

Karin agreed, and left Yolanda to send the rest of the family home. She would remain, she insisted, in case Lenora needed someone familiar.

Karin discovered she had no cell-phone reception in the parking garage, so she drove out and found a spot on the street.

The phone rang barely once, Bruce answering so quickly she knew he'd been waiting for her call.

"How is she?"

She described the visit and admitted how much she hadn't wanted to tell Lenora what had really happened. "Should I have?" she asked, feeling pitiful.

"No." His answer was decisive. "There's no escaping it, but you'll know when the time is right. Why are you questioning yourself? You have good instincts."

"Thank you," Karin said meekly. "How's your new case going?"

He and Molly had squeezed out the time to do the self-defense workshop at A Woman's Hand last night, but both had been obviously distracted. Bruce had given Karin a quick kiss afterward, and had gone.

"We're about to make an arrest. That means I'll be tied up all night with booking and reports." He paused. "I'd rather be with you."

A little shakily, she said, "I'd like to be with you, too. But I'm fine. It's good that you've caught the bad guy."

"I do occasionally." He sounded wry. "This was a drug-dealer turf war. No real victims. I'd rather catch Escobar."

"You will."

"I've got to go."

"Okay." The words *I love you* crowded her tongue, shocking her a little. They had come so close to escaping, as if they were something she said often, as commonly as goodbye.

What would he have said in return? she wondered.

"If I get a minute, I'll call you later," he said.

Pressing End and restoring her cell phone to her purse, Karin asked herself if that was the closest he would ever come to telling her he loved her. It was a way of saying that he cared, she supposed. Cold comfort.

What would happen when she let the words slip, as she inevitably must?

Of course she knew. That would send him running. After all, he'd warned her. He didn't fall in love, and he never intended to marry.

Making no effort to put her car in gear, Karin sat with her head resting back, her eyes closed.

I'm a fool, she thought unhappily. She should tell him and get it over with.

Sooner rather than later.

CHAPTER NINE

BRUCE WALKED into Lenora Escobar's hospital room on Thursday to find Karin was there before him. The curtains rattled as he pushed them aside.

Karin, sitting on the far side of the bed, gave him the quick smile that warmed someplace deep inside him. As always, she was beautiful, her corn-silk hair bundled up carelessly, baring the graceful length of her neck. She wore only gold hoops in her ears and a simple white tee that was almost, but not quite, an off-the-shoulder style. Even her collarbone was sexy to him.

He nodded back, then turned his attention to the other woman. Two days had passed since Lenora had opened her eyes and spoken to her sister. This morning, finally, her questions about her children had become so insistent Yolanda had begged Karin to be the one to tell Lenora the entire story.

"Hi, Lenora. I don't know if you remember me."

With the bed cranked to its highest setting, she sat nearly upright, wearing some kind of pink chenille robe that couldn't be hospital issue. Her head was still wrapped in a stiff white casing, but her face was unmarked by the trauma to the back of her head. He pictured her from that first workshop, a pretty, too-thin woman who'd then had a wealth of dark hair, presumably now shaved off.

She studied him with uncomfortable intensity. "I don't exactly remember, but… Maybe a little. I know your face." She glanced at Karin, then back at him. "Karin told me you led that class."

"Yes." He stood, his hands loosely wrapped around the top bar of the bed railing. "I wish it had done you some good."

She shook her head. "Roberto—he could be so mean. When he used to hit me, I never had time to duck. He was fast." Her hand lifted and jerked, an unnerving mimicry.

"Do you recall leaving him?"

Another shake. "I remember putting money away. I liked looking at him and planning how I was going to take the children and go."

"Karin's told you what Roberto did."

Grief suffused her face. "He killed Aunt Julia. She was like my mother. And…" Her voice faltered. "Anna and Enrico. He has them."

"He killed her to get them."

"He always said he wouldn't let me go." Her voice was duller now; she rolled her head against the pillow to speak to Karin. "You warned me not to tell him I was going. You said if I had someone with me, he'd hurt that person, too."

Surprised, Karin exclaimed, "I said that only a couple of days before you did take the kids and leave him."

Her forehead creased. "Then why don't I remember?"

"It's common," Bruce told her, "for someone who has a head injury like you do to have blocked out everything leading up to the trauma. It may be that part of you does remember. Deep inside, you know that the day you left him was the beginning."

"If I'd stayed…"

"Sooner or later, he was going to hurt you just as bad," Karin said firmly.

"I was afraid…" she whispered.

"That he'd hurt the children, too."

"Yes." She was now frantic, and her gaze swung back to Bruce. "Why can't you find them? He can't take care of Enrico and Anna!"

"I'm hoping you can give us some ideas about where he might have gone."

"I don't know! How can I?"

Karin leaned forward and laid a gentle hand on Lenora's. "You know him, Lenora. Detective Walker just hopes you can tell him about Roberto's friends, maybe places he's been."

"I understand his mother recently returned to Mexico," Bruce said. "Do you think he would take the kids and follow her?"

"I don't know! He was angry at her for going back. And his mother—she'd ask where I am."

"We've contacted police in Chiapas. They've talked to her and to her other son. Roberto's brother," he said in an aside for Karin's benefit, "has promised to phone if they hear from him." The officer with whom Bruce had spoken wasn't sure the mother would betray Roberto, but the brother seemed to be angry with him.

"He always said how much better it was here." Lenora moved fretfully. "I don't think he would want to go back to Mexico."

"Did he ever follow the harvests, like your sister and her family?"

"No. When he first came to this country, Roberto worked building houses. He was always good at building. He could make more money doing that than he could picking apples or asparagus."

When coaxed, she told them that Roberto had stolen into the United States illegally, paying a coyote one thousand dollars to smuggle him inside a truck over the border. Roberto had lived in Los Angeles at first, but he didn't like it there, so he had gotten a ride with other immigrants north. He had stopped in Sacramento, then gone briefly to Idaho before ending up in Seattle, where he got his green card following an amnesty offer.

"He always said he didn't like the other places. But sometimes he threatened to move us. He didn't like how much time I spent talking to Aunt Julia on the phone." Her face crumpled, and she whispered, "Is that why he killed her?"

Bruce wondered, too, picturing that day. Roberto had already hated his wife's aunt, and now the aunt had conspired to help Lenora escape him. She was trying to keep his children from him.

How Roberto thought was still more of a mystery to Bruce than he liked. Although filled with rage, Roberto had no ability to empathize or understand normal human emotions. He could hit his wife, then act as if nothing whatsoever had happened. Hot and cold. Which had he been when he'd murdered Julia Lopez? Fiercely glad to punish her for all the years in which she had, in his mind, encouraged Lenora to defy him? Or essentially oblivious to her existence as a human being? At that moment, had she been no more than an obstacle to him, one that needed eliminating?

"She had Enrico and Anna," Karin said simply. "She would never have let him take them if she could prevent it."

Lenora turned beseeching dark eyes on Karin. "Why was I so foolish? You said I shouldn't go near my family. I remember that. Why did I?"

Again, Karin squeezed her hand. "You wanted what was best for the kids. You told me they missed their aunt Julia and uncle Mateo. Staying close with family mattered. You thought they should know that some things hadn't changed."

"We should have gone away," she said dully. "As far away as we could. We should have gone before he could stop us."

"To leave and not be able to see your family— that's hard," Karin murmured. "You couldn't anticipate what he'd do."

"I always thought he'd kill me." Those eyes were haunted now. "I wanted to save Anna and Enrico. And now he has them."

She was too distraught to recall friends Roberto

might have had, or of any special places he might have talked about. She gave Bruce nothing new to work with. Seeing that he was only upsetting her, he told her to call him if anything occurred to her, and Karin walked with him into the hall.

They paused, out of earshot of the room behind them and the nurses' station ahead. "I'll try again later. When she calms down," Karin said.

"All right. Good. Call me if you come up with anything."

She nodded. "Did you ever find that friend he had at the lumberyard? Carlos?"

"Neither hide nor hair. My guess is, the last name at least was false, and he has new ID now. Stumbling over him may require pure luck."

"I wonder if Lenora will ever remember."

Aware of her distress, he touched her cheek. "It might be better if she doesn't."

"Yes. I suppose." She gave him a ghost of a smile. "Will you be by later?"

"Do you want to have dinner?"

"Mmm... Why don't I make something. I'm not sure I'm in the mood to go out."

"Would you rather I didn't come?"

He was startled when tears brimmed in her eyes just before she rose on tiptoe and kissed him quickly. "I would hate it if you didn't come," she said, her voice both fierce and a little desolate.

Two people emerged from a nearby room, and a nurse approached from the station. Bruce wanted to hold Karin, but after a glance at the other couple, who had begun a low-voiced conclave, he said only, "Then I'll be there."

That seemed to be enough; she nodded, and slipped back into Lenora's room.

He'd have hated it if she'd said tomorrow was fine. Walking away, he tried to figure out how he'd descended to this state, unable to get through a day without seeing her. No matter how good the sex was—and it was incredible—he knew damn well he'd be on her doorstep begging for her to let him in even if she'd taken a vow of celibacy. *She* drew him, body, mind and soul.

The common words people used to describe this powerful need crossed his mind, but he shoved them away. He couldn't deal with the implications. What he felt was an obsession, no more or less than the compulsion that gripped him when he was investigating a murder. At some point, he would be satisfied and ready to move on.

Until then…God help him, he couldn't get enough of her.

THIS SHOULD BE the slow season for murder in Seattle, but this past month Homicide was doing a brisk business for some reason. He and Molly had moved to the top of the list again, and within hours of him talking to Lenora in the hospital were called to a shooting that wasn't a mystery.

Two neighbors had been feuding for years, apparently; the last straw was when the victim let his dog, on the end of the leash, crap right in the middle of the neighbor's lawn, in plain sight of his front windows.

Then he petted the dog and started toward home. Walter Sims grabbed his handgun and roared out the front door, where after an exchange of "words"—described by yet another neighbor as a screaming match—he shot his neighbor of twenty-three years, Arthur Shearin.

After examining the body of the balding man, who had died wearing a worn white undershirt, ancient polyester slacks and bedroom slippers that exposed bony ankles, Molly and Bruce straightened and looked toward Sims, sitting in the back of a squad car. He had the downy white hair of a dandelion. She shook her head. "Wouldn't you think they were old enough to know better?"

Sims was in his late sixties, Shearin seventy-one according to their DMV records. Both were widowed. Maybe if their wives had lived, they'd have injected some sense in their husbands. Although Bruce had his doubts. It sounded as if the two men had reveled in their bitter relationship.

"Any next of kin?" he asked.

The uniform standing nearby said, "Woman two doors down says he has a daughter. She visited about once a week."

Sims had already been read his rights and sat unbowed in the back seat, his eyes ablaze with something like fanaticism when Bruce and Molly spoke with him.

"I had a restraining order against him," he snapped. "I had a right to defend myself when he trespassed."

"Sidewalks are city property," Molly observed. "Did he actually step into your yard?"

They knew from a witness that Shearin hadn't. What he'd done was stand on the sidewalk but allow the dog to go to the far length of the retractable leash to do his business on the velvety swath of lawn.

"I was supposed to turn a blind eye to his never-ending provocations? There's a law against harassment."

Bruce knew better than to think this cantankerous old man would ever feel remorse or even a twinge of self-doubt. Both of them, stubborn and filled with hate, had played their parts in a drama as inevitably tragic as *Othello* or *Hamlet*.

Once again, Bruce and Molly spent their day on booking, arraignment and reports. The worst part was visiting the daughter, once they found her name in a search of the home, to tell her that her only remaining parent had been shot dead by his next-door neighbor.

Finally, on Friday, Bruce was able to follow up on an idea that had come to him. Leaving Molly making phone calls on a cold case they'd never quite given up on, he went back to the lumberyard where Escobar had worked. Upon his arrival, the supervisor hurried from the back, appearing less than thrilled to be visited by the policeman again.

"A picture of Carlos Garcia?" His expression suggested that Bruce was crazy. "We wouldn't have any reason to have something like that."

"I'm hoping you can ask your employees. Someone might have brought a new digital camera into work and snapped pictures for the hell of it."

"Why would they have kept one of some guy who didn't even work here that long?"

"Because he was standing next to someone else?"

He grunted, then raised his voice. "Marge? Can you come here for a minute?"

Marge was the middle-aged cashier who, during Bruce's last visit, had recalled the friendship between the two men.

Entering the office, she said, "Detective Walker. Have you found those children yet?"

The *Seattle Times* had moved on to other stories now, but workers here must have pored over the front-page news about a crime that had awakened public sympathy because of the missing children.

"No, and that's why I'm back. I'd like to find any friends Roberto might have had."

"Didn't we tell you everything we knew about Carlos?" she asked, looking to the supervisor.

He shrugged. "He wants to know if we might have a picture of the guy."

"I think we do," she said, to both their surprise. "Not a very good one, because it was of all of us, but not that long ago I was noticing he was in it."

It turned out to have been taken as part of the business's fiftieth-anniversary celebration. All the employees had been lined up in front of a pile of lumber, a panel truck with the lumberyard name, logo and phone number parked beside them. An eight-by-ten, it had been framed and hung, forgotten and gathering dust, in the office.

Sure enough, when Bruce peered at it, he saw that next to Roberto was another Hispanic man, mustachioed, as well, of a similar age. He was a hand span taller, with a beaklike nose that might make him easily recognizable.

"May I borrow the picture?" Bruce requested. "I'll get it back to you."

"Sure, sure," the supervisor said. He'd stood beside Bruce, peering at it, as well, in some bemusement. "Can't believe I never noticed this, even after you were here asking about Roberto and Carlos."

Bruce went straight to a nearby photo shop, where he explained that he wanted a close-up of the two men only, and was told to come back in an hour. The nearest fast food was Kentucky Fried Chicken, where he ate and brooded.

A hunch was a funny thing. Why was his gut telling him that Carlos Garcia was the key? There were still a couple of other maybe friends of Escobar's whom he hadn't located, but he didn't feel the same urgency about them. He suspected it had something to do with Marge's observations being so astute. By God, if she'd imagined a bond between the two men, Bruce would put money on the fact that one existed. He'd told her today that if she ever wanted a change of career, she ought to apply to the Seattle PD. She'd laughed merrily, but he hadn't been altogether kidding. If more officers were anywhere near as observant as she was, there'd be less crime in the Emerald City.

But Bruce's gut instinct wasn't enough to justify calling on the newspapers to print the picture with an appeal to the public. Carlos Garcia, under any name, was no more than a person of potential interest. Realistically, if they did find him, he'd probably frown in perplexity and say, "Roberto Escobar? *Sí*, I worked with him, but I saw him only at the lumberyard."

Bruce was also reluctant to make Escobar feel cornered. He decided finally to distribute the photo to Hispanic grocery stores, community centers and medical clinics. Sympathy, he thought, would be with Lenora, not her husband. The biggest problem was that illegal immigrants were reluctant to come forward, especially given the recent federal crackdown and multiple deportations. Fear might keep silent people who'd like to help. But it was worth a try; a single call, saying, "I know that man," would make all the difference. And they'd be more likely to talk to him than to any federal agent.

He knocked off for the day without going back to the station because he was taking Trevor out for their usual pizza and maybe, with the lengthening daylight, to shoot some hoops. He hadn't gotten together with him since last week, when they'd gone to the Mariners game. Apparently, Dad was okay with the outing, because Trevor had dropped the phone and, after going off to consult him, had said, "Cool," in answer to the invitation.

After Bruce picked him up, they decided to shoot hoops at the local middle school before going out to eat. During the drive, and as they took turns dribbling the basketball along the paved exterior walkways to the hoops in back of the school, Bruce noticed that the boy was unusually quiet.

Bruce had asked once how things were going, and gotten the usual shrug and, "Okay."

He decided not to push it for now. They played one-on-one and then horse, with Bruce handicapping himself. The kid was developing a hell of an outside shot and not a bad layup, considering his height.

"I think you've suddenly grown," Bruce said. "At least an inch."

"You think?" Trevor asked eagerly.

"Your jeans are short."

They both gazed down at the exposed white sweat socks.

"Cool! Except I look like a geek."

He didn't sound as if he cared, not yet having expressed any interest in girls.

"I doubt your dad will mind buying you a couple of new pairs of jeans," Bruce said mildly.

Trevor's face closed and he shrugged, then began dribbling the ball in place, his head bent and his concentration absolute. He didn't want to talk about his dad.

Or else he did, and felt disloyal.

"You hungry?" Bruce asked.

"Yeah, I guess so."

"Why don't we head on back to the car, then."

The boy nodded and dribbled the way they'd come.

Bruce made a feint and stole the ball. "Hey!" Trevor cried, and raced after him, managing to knock it away. By the time they reached the car, they were both breathless and laughing.

They played some arcade games while they waited for their pizza. Not until they were eating did Bruce say, in a neutral tone, "I'm guessing your dad did something that upset you."

After a quick, startled glance, Trevor hunched his shoulders. "Maybe."

"You want to tell me about it?"

He took a piece of pizza and severed a strand of cheese. He took a bite, apparently not intending to answer at all. Finally, he mumbled, "It wasn't that bad."

Anger tightened in Bruce's chest. "It?"

Trevor poked at a congealing strand of cheese on his plate and said barely audibly, "He kinda got mad."

"At you?"

"I guess so." He spoke down to the plate. "Or maybe at Mom. I'm not sure."

"Mom?" What the hell? Bruce thought. Had Mary-Beth called or appeared and no one had told him?

"I was talking about her, and how much I miss her and stuff. You know?" Trevor risked a glance up. "And he grabbed her picture from me and threw it against the wall." Tears filled his eyes. "The glass broke, and the picture got ripped. And it was my favorite!"

That son of a bitch.

Bruce had remembered the framed photo. It was one of several MaryBeth had hung in the hall at their apartment. Most were Trevor's school pictures, and there were a couple of mother and son together. Bruce remembered one that included Wade, although it showed his back as he tossed a delighted Trevor, maybe five, up in the air. But the one of MaryBeth had been taken by a friend, she'd told Bruce, and in it she was laughing and startlingly pretty, free of the strain of financial worries and drug abuse that had later aged her face. For Trevor, the photo was irreplaceable, and by God he had so little to treasure.

Tamping down his fury, determined not to frighten Trevor, Bruce asked, "Has your dad been drinking?"

Trevor sniffed, swiped at his eyes with the hem of his T-shirt and shook his head. "Uh-uh."

"Did he talk to you about why he broke the picture?"

"He came in after I went to bed and said he was sorry and he'd try to fix it. But I don't think he can."

"He didn't hit you?"

"Uh-uh. He just really scared me. It just made me remember how mad he used to get. That's why Mom didn't want me ever to see him again."

Bruce nodded, but made himself add, "Everyone gets mad sometimes, though. Don't you?"

"I would've liked to punch Jackson."

Bruce half laughed. "Yeah. I know what you mean."

"Did you ever punch anybody?"

"I got in fights a few times back when I was a kid."

"I bet you won, 'cuz you're strong."

"I wasn't then. I got beaten up pretty good when I was a freshman in high school." One of the worst days of his life, and he'd shut out the memory for years. "My father was angry at me because I lost the fight."

Seeing Trevor's interest, he wished he hadn't said that.

"But...you couldn't help it!" the boy protested.

"My father thought being a real man meant using your fists." *Pansy* and *coward* were the mildest things his father had called him.

Clear as day, Bruce recalled sitting at the kitchen

table quailing from his father, who bent over him with a flushed, furious face, yelling, "Haven't I taught you anything? You make me sick, boy."

Having his own father stare at him with disgust, as if he'd proved his worthlessness, had hurt more than his throbbing eye or bloody nose. And yet, even then, inside he'd rebelled. He hadn't had the courage to say, *You didn't teach me to fight. You taught me to get beat up and not cry about it,* but he'd wanted to. Oh, he'd wanted to.

"That's why you don't like my dad," Trevor surprised him by saying. "Right?"

Hole in one. But, remembering his promise to the caseworker, Bruce said, "I don't know your dad well enough yet to like him *or* to dislike him. We both need to give him a chance."

"He scared me," Trevor said again.

"I can tell." Bruce looked him in the eye. "Will you promise to tell me if he does again?"

Trevor hesitated, then nodded.

It wasn't quite a promise, but Bruce sensed it was as close as he'd get. Trevor hadn't been sure tonight whether he should tell Bruce about the incident with his mother's framed photo, and the why wasn't hard to figure out. Trevor might not want to admit it, but he knew in his heart that his mother was gone from his life. In his eyes, Bruce had rejected him. In contrast, his dad not only wanted him—he was being good to him. Of course he felt disloyal complaining about him.

Bruce drove Trevor home and walked him to the front door, managing a civil nod at Wade.

But back in his car, he let his anger swell and even fed it with his memory of some of the things MaryBeth had told him. Trevor hadn't been back with Wade for more than a couple of weeks, and the son of a bitch was already up to his old tricks.

Bruce's fingers curled around the steering wheel, making the plastic creak.

Let that bastard lift his hand to Trevor once—just once—and by God he'd be sorry he was ever born.

That's why you don't like my dad, right?

Yeah, kid, Bruce thought. *That's exactly why I don't like your dad.*

CHAPTER TEN

"YOU LOOK LIKE something's bothering you," Karin observed.

It was Sunday, and Bruce had stopped by shortly after she'd gotten home from a morning visit to Lenora, who would be in the hospital for some time yet. Karin hadn't expected him, and could tell immediately that something was wrong. But when her heart jumped and she asked if he'd learned anything about Roberto or the children, he shook his head.

"Had another false alarm yesterday. Cop up in Skagit County reported a man who met Escobar's description, heading into a grocery store with two young children. Girl's hair wasn't very well braided, her clothes mismatched. The little boy was sobbing. The guy didn't seem to be an experienced parent." Bruce shrugged. "But it wasn't him."

Karin had been outside when he arrived, intending to work in the garden, and they'd ended up sitting on the porch steps in the sun. Roses and clematis were coming into bloom, their leggy stems disguised by a tumble of perennials. She loved this time of year, but the garden wasn't having its usual soothing effect. She kept seeing Lenora's haunted eyes, and now watched Bruce, wondering what had disturbed him.

He was slow answering her observation that wasn't quite a question. When he did, it was by indirection. "I took Trevor out for pizza last night."

She nodded; she'd known Bruce's plans.

"Wade's true character is coming out. He had a temper tantrum the other day."

"Oh, no," Karin said softly. "That poor boy! What happened?"

"The way I understand it, Wade got jealous because Trevor was talking about his mother too much. Wade grabbed the picture of his mom that Trev was holding and smashed it against the wall. Shattered the glass and damaged the photo. Trevor was pretty freaked."

"He didn't hurt Trevor, though?"

"Not this time." Bruce's tone was flat, anger simmering beneath it.

"Um…are you sure Wade was jealous?"

Incredulous, he turned to stare at her. "What do you mean? What else could it be?"

"Well…" Was this a good idea? Not at all sure, Karin picked her words carefully. "Could he be mad at MaryBeth? That is her name?" She glanced at him for confirmation.

Bruce didn't seem to notice. "*He's* mad at *her?* She protected Trevor with her own body when Wade lived with them, and since then she's scraped to make a living and care for Trevor."

"Didn't he pay child support?"

"When he got himself together enough to offer, she refused his money. She was afraid that if she cashed the son of a bitch's checks, it would give him rights."

In genuine puzzlement, Karin said, "But from what you tell me, the cupboards were bare some of the time! Did she consider that by turning down the child support—child support he was legally required to pay, visitation or no visitation—she was depriving Trevor?"

"You think she should have sacrificed her kid so she didn't have to get food stamps?"

The way he looked at her, with something like contempt, annoyed Karin enough that she ignored her better judgment and insisted on making her point. "I'm saying that if it's true Wade got alcohol treatment and went to anger-management classes, pulled his life together and offered child support, maybe he deserved a chance to maintain some contact with his son. Would he have done any of that if he didn't care?"

"How many chances does a bastard who beats his wife deserve?"

Karin shook her head. "I don't blame MaryBeth for not wanting him back. But that's not the same thing as acknowledging they shared a child."

He snorted. "From what I hear, Wade didn't share a damn thing but sperm. He was a loser. MaryBeth cut her losses and figured Trevor was better off without him."

"But in the end, he did need his dad, didn't he?"

"God! After this latest display, you still think that?"

Karin finally did hesitate. "Bruce, are you listening

to me? I haven't met Wade, and I won't pretend to guess whether he's capable of being the father Trevor deserves. But I do think that MaryBeth let Trevor down, and I can understand why Wade might have gotten angry if Trevor was talking about her as though she walked on water. That wasn't the right way for him to handle the situation. He should have understood how much Trevor must miss his mother, no matter what problems she had. But the fact is, by letting her drug addiction win, she may have done as much damage to Trevor as his dad did with his alcohol addiction."

Abruptly, Bruce rose to his feet, stalked a couple of feet down the walkway and then swung back to face her, his eyes glittering and his body so tense she was reminded of a boxer balancing on the balls of his feet, waiting for his opponent to launch an attack. "Why are you so determined to view him through rose-colored glasses? You were quick enough to condemn Escobar."

"Why are you so quick to condemn Trevor's father?" Karin retorted.

"Quick? I've read the hospital records and police reports after he battered MaryBeth."

She felt as if she'd wandered into a hall of mirrors, except that the distorted images she was seeing were of Bruce rather than herself. Did she know him at all? She sat stiffly, gripping the painted steps as though to orient herself.

"Then you don't believe in reformation."

"I know his type." Voice and expression were unrelenting. "They don't change."

"People can learn to manage their anger…"

He made a rude sound. "Pop psychology. The classes are a joke."

Now *she* was getting mad. "Is everything I do pop psychology, too?"

"I didn't say that."

"You might as well have. What I'm telling *you* is that people who are sufficiently motivated are capable of change."

"And you call shattering the kid's favorite picture of his mother *change?*"

"It might be." She knew she sounded brittle, knew that argument was hopeless, but she couldn't seem to stop herself. "In classes, participants are taught that if their anger is boiling over, as a last resort they should vent it on an object rather than a person. That might have been what Wade was doing. He didn't hurt Trevor. It's not good that he scared him, but—"

"God almighty. Why am I wasting my time talking to you about this? Enjoy your fantasy world, lady." He swung around and walked away.

Stunned, she realized he was leaving, thinking he'd had the last word. He'd dismissed every word she said.

Karin jumped to her feet and chased after him, catching up to him as he reached his car at the curb. "Where are you going?"

He slapped the top of the car and swung back to face her. The metal rang out, making her jump.

"To talk to the son of a bitch and tell him that if he lays one hand on his son, he's got me to answer to."

She lifted her chin and met his furious eyes. "After which, he'll slug you and you'll slug him and then… What? You'll arrest him for assaulting a police officer and be sanctimonious because you were right about him all along?"

He raised his voice, making sure the whole neighborhood heard him. "You spend your days with women who've been raped or had the shit beaten out of them, and you still can't admit there are vicious men out there who shouldn't be allowed within a hundred miles of their families?"

It came to her then in an insight she felt dumb for not having had sooner. "You don't just think *he's* like your father. You think *all* men are."

"Don't psychoanalyze me." He leaned toward her, eyes narrow slits, teeth showing. "I don't have anything to do with this. It's about Wade DeShon, and your naive refusal to believe he's anything but a good man who screwed up once. No, oops. Five or six times. Or was it ten? But he's taken a few classes, so he must be born anew."

His sarcasm, snarled at her from inches away, made her even madder and erased her last semblance of good judgment.

She poked him in the chest. "You know what your problem is? You've been playing at being Trevor's daddy. You *want* Wade to fail so you can dash to the rescue again. But you wouldn't make any real commitment to Trevor the last time, and I'm betting you won't the next time, either." She wound down, thought through what she'd said, then asked simply, "Why wouldn't you?"

"Because I can't be trusted any more than his father can!" he shouted.

They stared at each other, his face suffused with angry color, hers reflecting… She didn't know. Bewilderment? Shock? Certainly some anger, as well.

He'd said before that he hadn't learned to parent, and perhaps that he feared being too much like his father. It was true that child abuse did echo from generation to generation, so he had reason to be nervous. But to truly believe he'd lift his hand against a kid he'd done so much to help…?

Still stunned, she shook her head. "You *aren't* your father."

Without stepping back, he visibly retreated from her, pulling his head and shoulders back, stiffening. "I doubt there's a man alive who can be entirely trusted if pushed far enough. Me, I've had an example of what I can be like. I told you. I'm a carbon copy of my dear dad."

"Appearances don't mean anything!" she cried in frustration.

He shook his head. "I'm not fool enough to find out."

"My God," she whispered. "You really are afraid you'd hurt someone you loved, just because you got mad."

"I'm not going to find out."

The hope she'd hardly known she felt came close then to blinking out. She crossed her arms tightly over her chest in an instinctive effort to protect herself.

"Do you have any idea how big a fool I feel right this minute?" Tears burned in her eyes, but she refused to let them fall. "I didn't listen to you. I thought…I believed… No, I *deluded* myself that you might actually love me. But you can't."

His rigid demeanor shattered, and abruptly, he was shouting again. "Don't you understand? I don't dare!"

Her mouth fell open. It was a moment before she could close it. She swallowed, but her voice still emerged as thin and dry. "*Do* you love me?"

What she saw in his eyes was torment, but he said nothing. He wasn't going to answer her. Couldn't?

Weirdly, perhaps, his silence fed the small, stubborn spark in her chest that hadn't quite died. As if hope had been banked and not quenched, it flared again, the heat giving her courage.

"You're a coward," she accused him. "You've spent an entire lifetime avoiding any emotional commitment because you're afraid."

Muscles flexed in his jaw. "I made a decision…"

"No, you're a coward," she repeated. She took a step forward, crowding him, forcing him back against the side of his car. "You don't have the guts to find out whether you're capable of being a better man than your father. And then you condemn men who at least were willing to try and keep trying."

"Don't compare me with Wade DeShon," he hissed.

"Why not?" Karin hardly understood what drove her, then knew. Instinct. "I *am* comparing you, and right this minute, he looks pretty damn gutsy to me compared with you."

Bruce crowded her right back, so much anger on his

face a sensible woman would have quailed. "I told you not to compare me!"

She stabbed him in the chest again with one finger, hard this time. Her vision seemed hazed. With red? "But I'm doing it anyway," she all but crowed. "Wade DeShon had the guts to love someone, and he has the guts now to say, *I screwed up, but I still love you.* That looks a lot braver to me than opting out of any kind of real relationship because you won't even test yourself to find out whether you're just like your daddy or not!"

His eyes were all but black they were so dilated. "Do you want to find out? Is that what you really want?"

"Yes! That's what I want!" Karin yelled.

And then braced herself.

It was like facing down a volcano. She'd never been so aware of how powerful this man was, how heavy-boned and thick-muscled compared with what felt at this moment like her own frailty. He stared at her with those rage-darkened eyes, the hot blood of fury turning his face deep red.

The haze before Karin's eyes was gone, as if with one blink she'd swept it away. Instead, she now saw him with peculiar clarity. Nothing existed *but* this man, so furious with her, so afraid he would hurt her. Time stretched, thinned, as she waited for him to betray himself and strike her.

But his fingers never curled into a fist. He never raised a hand. He only stared, unblinking, not breathing. And finally, his expression changed. Shock was followed by bewilderment that wrenched her heart, so much did it remind her of a child who'd suddenly seen the world he had believed in transformed into something unrecognizable.

Karin's vision blurred again, but this time with tears she let fall. They rolled, hot, down her cheeks.

She laid one hand on Bruce's hard cheek. He made a muffled, agonized sound and turned his head to press his face into her hand, and she felt dampness. Oh, God. Was he crying, too?

"I'm sorry. I shouldn't have…" Her voice broke.

Yes! her heart sang. *Yes, you should have.*

His shoulders lurched.

Karin took her hand from his face and wrapped her arms around him. He leaned against her, buried his face in her hair and shook.

"Now are you convinced?" she murmured, rocking him and holding him with all her strength. "You didn't, you *couldn't,* hurt me. You never would."

Against her cheek, he said hoarsely, "I always believed… I thought I was *him.*"

"But now you know better." When he didn't answer immediately, she tried to pull back a few inches. "You do, don't you?"

He lifted his head and looked at her, his cheeks unashamedly wet. "Yeah. I think I do."

Her tears ran hotter. She smiled through them. "Will you come inside?"

GOD. He'd probably created a spectacle for the entire neighborhood. Earlier on, when he'd stomped to his car, Bruce had been vaguely conscious of a car passing, of a neighbor kid riding his bike on the sidewalk on the far side of the street. His head had swiveled so he could gawk at the two adults yelling at each other.

But Karin didn't seem to care. Through the tears that rained down her face, she shone. Always beautiful, now she was incandescent. He'd be a fool if he *didn't* love her.

Bruce yanked himself up short. It was too quick to consider labeling some emotion he'd never been able to name. What he should think about was what he'd just learned about himself.

He'd always been aware of a core of anger inside him. No, not just anger; something blacker than that, something that scared even him. A violent, monstrous emotion. It had been there as long as he could remember. He kept it in a closed room inside him, locked down. But locks could be broken, walls splintered. Even as a little boy, when he watched his father hit his mother, Bruce would feel the scary emotion swelling until he didn't think he could keep it contained.

He'd also known his whole life that his ability to control the demon that lived inside him was all that made him different from the father he despised. He'd descend to his father's level if he ever once loosed the violence. Bruce had come close a few times, mostly as a young man. He had dreamed about beating his father bloody, about making him crawl. But never, until today, had he felt those walls crash down, felt the fury swell inside him until he was filled with it, sweated it through his pores, was blinded by it.

And now, finally, he knew. He could feel monstrous emotions and not *be* a monster. All the rage his body could contain hadn't made him want to hurt her. Not even for a fraction of a second had he longed to snap her head back with one blow of his hand. He hadn't thought, *I want to see her on her knees, sobbing how sorry she is.*

And somehow, she'd had faith in the man he really was. She had trusted him.

Humbled to the core, Bruce had been shaking when he held her even as she held him. He felt as if he should be embarrassed to have shed tears, but wasn't. He took her hand, likely crushing her fingers when he gripped hard enough not to lose her, and walked the few feet from the street up her walkway, across the porch and into the house.

The moment the door shut behind them, she flung herself against him and his arms wrapped around her with a force he tried to keep from bruising her. The receding tide of anger left in its wake a desperate need to be so close to this woman she could never deny him. A need to be on top of her. Inside her. He wanted their very cells to be united.

An incoherent sound wrenched from him. He bent his head and captured her mouth. Dimly, he was aware that she was kissing him back as frantically, that she'd risen on tiptoe and wound her arms around his neck and was pressing herself against him, feeling the same need. He fell against the door, then at some point spun her so her back was ground against it. He hoisted her, and her legs wrapped around him. She rode him as he plumbed the depths of her mouth and sucked on her tongue.

Bruce thought he might explode if he didn't feel her skin against his. He had to break off the kiss long enough to tear her shirt over her head. He was talking; he could hear himself, a litany that involved praying, swearing, saying her name as if it were the sweetest word ever formed. She seemed to be laughing or crying—he didn't know which—but she yanked at his clothing with hands as desperate as his.

They didn't get it all off. The sight of her body, long and pale and curvaceous, shredded his last bit of self-control. He lifted her, felt her legs clasp him willingly and drove inside. Arms shaking with the strain, he pushed her back against the door and thrust, over and over and over, a madman, not stopping even when her entire body convulsed around him and she keened. Not stopping until she did it again and he found his own release in a mind-splitting explosion of pleasure so acute it might have been pain. An explosion that did finally empty him, so that his knees began to buckle and he sank with her in slow motion to the hardwood floor.

Bodies still joined, they lay as close together as it was humanly possible to be. Almost numb, he knew only that he didn't want to let her go, that he didn't *care* how hard the floor was or whether he could breathe.

Sensations, irritating and unwelcome, intruded nonetheless. The floor was damn cold under his bare ass. His penis slipped from her, however he willed it to keep them linked. He became aware of a few places that stung. Her nails must have dug into his back and shoulders. He had a memory of her head banging against the door. God. Was she hurt?

Bruce groaned muzzily and raised his own head from the floor enough to allow him to see her face. Her cheek was slack. A lock of hair lay across it and trailed into her mouth. As he watched, she scrunched her face up, as if trying to regain muscle control.

"Are you okay?" It came out as a mumble. Hell, he hadn't been sure he could talk at all.

"Um…" Karin wet her lips. "I think so." She sounded uncertain, but suddenly, she lifted her head so she could see him better. "You?"

"Alive," he allowed.

Anxious eyes searched his. "Do you think we ought to get up?"

"Probably."

They didn't. Her head sagged back to his chest. He managed to make one hand move so he could stroke from her shoulder blades down the length of her spine to the swell of her buttocks. Vertebra to vertebra. Muscles quivered as his hand passed. He felt a stirring in the groin. Could he get aroused again?

Yeah, it seemed he could. But this time the urgency was lacking. He continued to stroke, not moving otherwise. Karin shifted against him finally and said, "I'm too old for the floor."

A laugh rumbled from deep in his chest. It delighted him that he could laugh.

When they finally did get up, man, things hurt. He

felt as if he'd been beaten up. He also saw the shadow of new bruises on her white flesh, but she said something he thought was "Pshaw" when he began an apology, and drew him by his hand into her bedroom.

The bed was a hell of a lot more comfortable than the hardwood floor had been. They lay down and touched, carefully this time, tenderly, as if seeing each other and exploring for the first time. Sex this time was slow and sweet and, yeah, damn it, loving.

But still he shied from the word. He didn't say it and she didn't say it. Maybe it wasn't necessary.

Or maybe, he thought at one point, studying her face, which seemed to him exquisitely shaped, maybe he was still afraid.

A lifetime's conditioning… Not so easily overcome. Yeah. He was still afraid.

CHAPTER ELEVEN

BRUCE SPOTTED Wade DeShon before Wade noticed him. They'd agreed to meet at Dick's near the Key Arena. Already sitting down, Wade had a drink and a bag in front of him, presumably containing his burger, but he hadn't started eating.

His head turned, and the two men exchanged stares, then brief nods. Bruce got in the too-lengthy line and inched forward. He didn't once glance back.

Why did Wade want to talk to him without Trevor around?

He'd been the one to call Bruce, not the other way around. Since the scene with Karin on Saturday, Bruce had stayed away. He still wasn't sure he bought her theory about Wade, the one that conceded him permission to smash the kid's favorite picture of his mother right in front of him. But Bruce had had to concede that he hadn't been prepared to give Wade any slack at all. And yeah, people screwed up. So maybe he'd jumped to a conclusion.

Which wasn't to say that he trusted the guy any more than ever.

The call, though, had been from out of the blue. Hearing the reason for it was going to be interesting.

He carried his own order to the table and sat facing Wade. Deliberately, in no hurry, he uncapped his coffee and stirred in the creamer, then opened the sack and removed the bag of fries and wrapped burger. Then he looked up.

"So, I'm here."

Wade set down his burger and wiped his hands on a napkin. To his credit, he didn't beat around the bush. "Trevor told me he talked to you about my breaking that picture."

"Yeah. He did."

"I wanted to explain."

Bruce took another bite, chewed slowly. Not until he'd swallowed did he say, "Then explain."

"He kept saying he knew something bad had happened to his mom, because she would have come home otherwise. He said she'd never have left him that way if she could help it."

Bruce hadn't intended to step in this quick, but he said, "I think that's true."

"MaryBeth loved Trevor—I won't deny that. But she wasn't any kind of perfect mother, either."

Speaks the perfect father.

On the heels of the snide judgment, Bruce could imagine Karin pinning him with an exasperated stare. *Listen to him,* she would say.

So he did his best to hide his hostility and kept eating.

"I boozed, but she liked uppers. It made me mad that

she used back when she was pregnant with Trevor. I'm not excusing myself. Not for my drinking, not for hitting her. But our fights weren't all me, either. Trevor doesn't remember that."

Wade would say that, Bruce reflected cynically. But he still kept quiet because he remembered that from the first time he'd met MaryBeth, he'd known she had a problem. Plus, while men did abuse women who never fought back—Bruce's mother was one of those—that wasn't what Trevor had described. He'd told of raging battles between MaryBeth and Wade.

"I have this feeling you've already made up your mind." Wade shrugged, looking defeated but determined, too. "I'm going to say this anyway. I got mad because she let him down so bad. I let him down, too. I know I did. But I saw him crying, and I thought he was doing all right without me, but having his mama just disappear like that… Him having to go to a foster home, and then come live with me when he doesn't even know me anymore… I could see in his eyes how scared and sad he was at that moment, and I lost my temper. I wasn't mad at Trevor. Not even just at MaryBeth. I was mad at myself, too. And I grabbed that picture and threw it before I thought, even though I believed I'd learned better. But I want you to know I wouldn't hurt him. I'd never hurt Trevor."

"Am I supposed to be moved by that little speech?"

Wade stared at him in frustration, then crumpled his wrappers in a little ball and started to stand. "Forget it."

"Sit down." Bruce put some snap in his voice.

After a hesitation, the other man complied.

"Maybe you mean that right now, but what happens the next time you crave a drink?"

Wade held Bruce's gaze, a mask dropping enough to reveal torment. "I crave a drink every day. Sometimes it's all I can stand not to have one. Just one, I tell myself. Only, I know better. So I don't have it. I haven't had one in over two years. If I can resist temptation that guts a man's soul for that long, what makes you think I'd give in to it now, when I finally got my son back?"

Bruce shoved the remnants of his lunch away. Despite himself, this time he *was* moved. Wade had been more eloquent than he would have expected. Karin had been right; Bruce didn't want to be impressed. But he was anyway.

"Why are you telling me all this?" he asked. "Why are we having this conversation?"

Wade looked back at him with a man's version of Trevor's thin, earnest face. "If you don't trust me, Trevor won't, either. At first, I was jealous." His mouth twisted. "But I don't have any right to be. The thing is, my boy admires you. So I guess I'm asking you to support my right to be his father. Let him see that you do."

He was begging, and last week that would have given Bruce satisfaction. He would have enjoyed the acknowledgment that he came first with Trevor. He might even have liked the idea of Wade crawling to him for help with his son.

Suddenly, he felt sick, ashamed of what just a few days ago he would have felt. Trevor wasn't his son. He could have been; if Bruce had been willing to make that commitment, trust himself, he could have been licensed as Trevor's foster father and fought any effort to reunite Trevor with his father. But Karin was on the mark. He hadn't had the guts to admit he loved the boy.

And now, *because* he loved him, he had to admit that Trevor was better off with his father. A kid that age needed to know that his parents, whatever their failings, loved him. That Wade had resisted the temptation to take that drink for more than two long years, even though he wasn't allowed to see his son, was a testament to how much he did love him. He'd kept calling, kept trying even when those calls weren't all that welcome. It was right that he get that second chance to show Trevor how much he mattered to his father.

"Do you want me to talk to him?" Bruce asked.

"Maybe. Or maybe just let him see that you approve of him living with me."

After a moment, Bruce said, "I have a friend who is a psychologist. She's been talking to me about her belief that people can change if they want to bad enough."

Wade was watching him, maybe wondering where this was going, maybe already knowing. "She's right. I've got to believe she is."

"I thought she was wrong. Just recently, I've started to change my mind." He paused. "Trevor didn't want to admit it, but back when you used to call, it meant something to him. He pretended he didn't care, but he did."

Wade lowered his gaze. He rubbed a hand over his face, pressing his thumb and forefinger to his eyes as if to make sure they didn't leak. At last, he cleared his throat. "I appreciate you saying that."

"I'll talk to Trevor." Bruce shifted in his plastic chair. "I hope you don't mind if I keep getting together with him now and again. He's a great kid."

"Of course I don't. You got him through some bad times. I owe you."

They eyed each other a little uneasily, dangerously close to emotions Wade probably didn't welcome any more than Bruce did. Finally, Bruce nodded and finished wadding up his garbage.

Wade thanked him for agreeing to meet and they walked out together. They even shook hands beside Wade's car, sealing their agreement.

We will both make things right for Trevor.

BRUCE REMAINED thoughtful as he spent the remainder of the afternoon dropping off flyers with photos of Carlos Garcia and Roberto Escobar at Hispanic grocery stores in south King County. His fluency in Spanish was handy now. At each stop he talked for a few minutes, reassuring the proprietors that he had no interest in the immigration status of anyone who came forward with information. He wanted only to find the children. He talked about Lenora's heartbreak, drawing a picture of the distraught woman in the hospital bed begging him to find her little ones, of the circle of her family waiting to regather the children into their arms.

The storekeepers all nodded and promised to post his

flyer and point it out to their customers. None cried, "I know that man!"

He'd done the Seattle metropolitan area one day, Snohomish County another day and the agricultural and heavily Hispanic Skagit County on yet another day. His lieutenant was becoming impatient with the time he was expending. As newspaper interest in the search for Anna and Enrico Escobar cooled even further—and therefore pressure from the public and from the politicians—so, too, did Bruce's ability to remain focused on the case.

His last stop of the day was in Kent, at a tiny store where several customers and the proprietor at the checkout were carrying on an animated conversation in Spanish, all gesticulating, until he entered. The moment the bell over the door rang and they saw him, they all fell silent and studied him covertly.

The atmosphere wasn't quite hostile, but almost. One of the men said loudly, "We can't even buy tortillas without showing our papers?"

"I'm not from Immigration," Bruce said, unoffended. He understood the unease in the Hispanic community. Recent immigration raids had angered many. Mothers in the country illegally had been torn from their children born in the U.S.—thus citizens—and deported. "I'm from the Seattle Police Department," he told them. "I'm investigating the murder of Julia Lopez and the attempted murder of Lenora Escobar. I am hunting for Lenora Escobar's young children, taken by her husband."

Their expressions changed. They'd all read about the case, talked about it among themselves.

"This man—why would we here know him?" asked the storekeeper, a short, stout, dark-skinned woman who had to be Mayan.

"We have no idea where he went with the children. It could be this area. I brought a picture of Roberto Escobar. But I'm also looking for the man beside him in the picture." He handed it over to her. "He is a friend of Escobar's. Not a suspect. But he might know where to find Roberto Escobar and the children."

All nodded interestedly and crowded closer to study the flyer. The storekeeper handed it across the old-fashioned counter holding a cash register that was probably an antique. With murmurs and clucking sounds, they passed the piece of paper around. It was greeted with shakes of the head.

No, no, they had never seen those men. What a shame. Those poor children! So the mother had awakened? They hadn't read that in the papers. It was true?

Answering their questions, he caught an interesting reaction out of the corner of his eye. It was from a woman, one of the last to look at the flyer. She composed her face immediately and shook her head like the others. But there'd been something there. Perhaps just niggling recognition, but she'd definitely known something and chosen not to say *I might have seen this man before.*

Question was: Which man had she recognized? Carlos? Or Roberto himself? And how to find out?

He grabbed a bottle of grape Fanta, paid and then stood in the shade outside, guzzling it until the woman emerged from the store with a younger woman—her daughter?—and her groceries.

"Buenos días," he said civilly.

"Buenos días," they chimed in return.

"You're certain you don't know either of those men?" he asked. "That Roberto Escobar… We think he's *loco*. Those two little kids aren't safe with him."

"No, no," the young woman said, and her mother nodded.

"If you should see either, will you call me? My phone number is on the flyer."

Sí, sí. Of course they would. The older woman's gaze evaded his. She hustled her daughter away. They loaded their groceries in the back of an old Chevy and drove off. Bruce jotted down the license number.

When he ran it from his car, he found that it was registered to a Vicente Sanchez at an address on the outskirts of Kent. Bruce debated with himself whether it would be worth following her home and talking to her husband and any other family who lived with them, then decided not to. The woman hadn't seemed secretive so much as unsure. He'd give her time to think about the flyer and why the face had seemed familiar, to imagine how she'd feel if her children or grandchildren were snatched from her.

The odds were good that she'd be calling him.

"Yeah," he muttered, putting his car in gear, "assuming she doesn't get home and realize that Carlos resembles some distant cousin of her husband's, the one who still lives back home in the Dominican Republic, and that's why she thought for a minute she might know him."

Feeling the stirrings of hunger, he detoured to a small Mexican restaurant down the street and had a chicken chimichanga. He left a flyer there, too. The waitress, who had been flirting with him, promised she would hang it prominently by the cash register. *Sí, sí.*

He made it back to Seattle in time to meet Molly at A Woman's Hand to teach their last self-defense workshop. Karin engaged as fully in it as the other women participants did, her expression often fiercely concentrated. He suspected that seeing Lenora brought down with one swing of the tire iron had made her aware of her own vulnerability in a way she never had been. It had occurred to her that she might have to defend herself someday, too.

Three weeks, and no progress at all in finding Roberto Escobar or the children.

After escorting the women safely to their cars, he, Molly and Karin went out again for coffee. He was glad Karin and Molly seemed to like each other so much. He'd had his doubts three years back when Molly, newly promoted, was assigned to him, but she'd proved herself with smarts he'd come to believe complemented his own *because* she was a woman and therefore thought differently. As plainclothes homicide officers, the two of them rarely had to chase suspects or pull a weapon. Her ability to bring down a violent suspect holding a knife on them wasn't often put to the test. But Molly had learned every trick to compensate for her lack of height and muscle bulk. Underestimating her was a mistake.

Friendship had grown between them. She'd hung out with him and Trevor a few times. Trevor's shyness hadn't lasted long with her. Molly wasn't girlie. She ate with gusto, took pride in her belches and employed a wicked elbow on the basketball court.

"Did you ever play basketball?" he asked Karin.

Both women turned their heads to stare at him.

"Uh…sorry. Did I interrupt?"

"Yeah," Molly told him. "Good to know you were hanging on our every word."

"I actually did play varsity in high school," Karin said. "I went to a small school, and we were pretty lousy, but I can dribble the ball and I used to have a pretty decent jump shot. Why?"

"Oh, just thinking." He shrugged. "Molly and I play a little one-on-one sometimes."

"Really?" Karin raised her brows and looked at his partner. "You're short."

Molly's blue eyes narrowed. "Bet I can take you."

Karin laughed. "No fair! I haven't played in fifteen years."

Bruce sipped coffee. "You didn't play in college?"

"Too busy by then. And really…I was no more than okay."

Walking her to her car later, Bruce murmured, "You may stink on the court, but you have other talents."

She rolled her eyes at him. "Gee, thanks. Like guiding people toward understanding their own behaviors?"

"That's what I was talking about," he agreed, straight-faced.

Her elbow in his ribs was damn near as sharp as Molly's.

She unlocked her car door and turned to him. "We didn't get a chance to talk about your meeting with Wade."

"He wants my support."

She processed that. "And does he have it?"

"If he doesn't screw up."

"Ah. Wholehearted, then."

"Damn it," he said with some heat, "I'm trying."

Karin rose on tiptoe and kissed him softly. "I know you are," she murmured.

He caught her to him and deepened the kiss long enough to make it really interesting, and to make him regret that he hadn't planned to go home with her tonight.

But when he let her go, she said meditatively, "I'd love to meet Trevor. What if we do a barbecue or something and invite him and his dad? Maybe Molly, too. Is there anyone else?"

He reacted with surprise and pleasure. He liked the idea of getting her opinion on Wade. Bruce was willing to bet she had x-ray vision that cut through any pretense. "I'd like that."

They discussed days, and agreed he'd call Wade.

"I'll let you know," he said, kissed her again, and reluctantly let her get into her car.

WHEN BRUCE CALLED Karin the next day to inform her that Saturday afternoon would work fine for Wade and Trevor, he told her more about his lunchtime meeting with Trevor's father. After she hung up, Karin found herself hoping that Wade was sincere. Given how angry Bruce had been, how certain he was that Wade was a brute beyond redemption, these were big steps for him. If it turned out badly, if Wade DeShon started drinking or lost his job and took out his frustration on his son, Bruce's tentative faith in the ability of any man to prove himself would collapse.

She was afraid of any new hitches because she'd noticed that despite his breakthrough, he had been very careful not to say the words *I love you.* Karin was trying not to think about the possibility that he *didn't.* That he might be willing to believe he could love a woman someday but she wasn't that woman.

Because the truth was, she had fallen head over heels in love with him. She missed him every minute when they weren't together, was giddy with her love when they were. It was like being tipsy for hours on end. She laughed more than she ever had in her life, was sillier than she'd been at twelve years of age, and had begun to dream about things she hadn't known how desperately she wanted: a huge church wedding, a bulging belly beneath a T-shirt that said Baby On Board, storytimes and family picnics and a vacation to Disneyland. PTA meetings, stolen romance with her husband, dinners out when they discovered all they talked about was their children. Normal stuff. Stuff she'd once assumed she'd have someday, but that in recent years she had almost forgotten she wanted.

But even if Bruce did love her, even if someday he said the words, would he ever want to make a lifetime commitment? Would he trust himself enough to father children? She didn't know, and that scared her. Discovering she'd fallen in love alone would be bleak.

She still went daily that week to see Lenora, who was making good progress. Initially, her speech had been better than her motor skills. Some of that was weakness from the weeks of inactivity, but not all. Like someone who'd had a stroke, much of the damage was one-sided. She'd retained more dexterity on her left side than her right. During visits, she told Karin about the physical therapy and about the things she could do effortlessly and the ones she was having to relearn like a newborn child. The bandage on her head became smaller, exposing scalp with a newborn's peach fuzz of dark hair.

One day she returned from the bathroom, walking with a stiff, awkward gait, climbed into bed with Karin's help and burst into tears.

"Anna loved my hair!" she wailed. "She liked to brush it and put her barrettes in. What would she say?"

"That you're as pretty as that singer with the bald head. Sinéad O'Connor."

She must have heard of her, because she laughed through her tears. "I thought she looked so funny when I saw a picture! A woman's hair should be beautiful."

Karin reached out and wiped away her tears. "I think your hair will be beautiful again. And Anna will brush it again, and style it for you. And Enrico will wonder why girls like to mess with their hair."

Lenora cried some more. Karin moved to the edge of the bed and held her as she wept against Karin's shoulder. Her own cheeks grew damp as she thought about how long it had been since Roberto smashed his wife's head with all that weekend's pent-up rage and stole the children not for their sakes but to prove they were *his*. What if they were never found? How would Lenora live not knowing? Looking for the rest of her life at the faces of other people's children, wondering, hoping, fearing?

Bruce hadn't conceded defeat. But eventually, he would have done everything that was possible. Other mysteries would preoccupy him. Other tragedies, other missing children. Not all *were* found. Karin had counseled women who'd had a child die. That was hard enough, but there had been resolution of a sort. Those mothers had a grave to visit. They might forever ask themselves if they couldn't have done something differently, but at least they knew the end.

Lenora might not. Would she be able to bear living with that uncertainty?

Karin went home depressed. As she got ready for bed, she thought about Trevor, whose mother had disappeared. For all that he knew his mother was a drug addict, it must be hard for him to understand her disappearance. Karin hoped that Wade would be willing to let him talk about his mother sometimes. She'd have to urge Bruce to encourage him to do so, too.

THE WEATHER SATURDAY, blessedly, was nice. Bruce had taken her literally when she suggested a barbecue, and brought his own kettle-type grill. He arrived early and started the coals. Karin was letting him prepare the meat for the grill. She was secretly amused by his expertise in this traditionally manly form of cooking.

Since she neither cooked nor ate meat, he'd promised to handle that whole part of the menu. Everything else would be vegetarian, from the baked beans to the salads.

She'd invited a couple who were good friends of hers, and Molly brought a date who had a boy nearly Trevor's age. Wade and Trevor were the last to arrive, and showed up with a case of soda and several bags of chips. She led them through the house to the back patio.

"Bruce is just putting the meat on," she told them over her shoulder. She peered in the bag Trevor had handed her. "Oh, you brought dip to go with the chips. That looks great."

Bruce grinned at the sight of the boy and held out a free hand for a quick hug. Understandable envy flashed on Wade's face before he veiled it. He had to compete not just with Trevor's memories of his mother, but with a man who'd stood in his place in his son's affections.

Molly greeted Trevor with casual affection and introduced him to the other boy. Bruce introduced Wade to everyone, and soon he and Karin's friend Steve discovered a common interest in old cars. Wade, it developed, was restoring a 1970 Camaro, which filled Steve with envy. They huddled, talking about its wheelbase and track and something about the subframe and structural integrity. Steve's wife rolled her eyes and offered to help Karin bring out the rest of the food.

Karin had only one private moment with Wade,

after they'd eaten, when she caught him standing apart from the others, watching Trevor and the other boy attempt to keep a soccer ball in the air with their knees and heads.

"He seems like a really nice kid," she said, pausing at his side.

He nodded. "Thanks to his mother. And Detective Walker," he added scrupulously.

"Bruce seems to think Trevor's settling in really well with you, though."

His face softened. "Yeah. Better than I expected. We've had some rough patches—" he gave her a sidelong glance, and she could tell he wondered how much she knew "—but he's doing good. Real good."

She bit her lip. "Has Bruce told you I'm a therapist?"

His appraisal was more frank this time. "He said he had a friend who was."

"Well, that was me." Here she went, butting in again. She couldn't seem to help herself. "Um…I'm wondering if I can give you a bit of advice."

Despite new wariness, he inclined his head. "Sure. I'm no expert at being a dad."

"It's not that," she said. "From what I've seen today, you're doing fine. I just have one suggestion. Encourage him to talk about his mother. The worst thing for a child is to have to pretend he never thinks about one of his parents. It happens often, after a divorce. Children do their best to please the parent they depend on. But if they stifle too much, it causes damage."

"Okay," he said after a minute. "I can do that. It used

to bother me, knowing that MaryBeth probably never said a good word about me."

"I imagine that made Trevor feel awfully conflicted, too, because on some level he loved you. It's really hard on a kid to have to betray one of his parents, in a sense, by having to agree that Mommy is mean and he never wants to see her again."

Wade nodded again, more thoughtfully. Then his expression changed, and she knew even without turning that Bruce had come up beside her.

He slipped an arm around her and said, "Has she said, 'Hmm—now, exactly what do you mean by that?' yet?"

Wade tried to hide his laugh in a cough. "Uh, not exactly."

"But close enough," Karin admitted. "I was dispensing advice. Just as bad."

Bruce grinned at her. "Just as long as you didn't say 'Hmm.' That's when you scare me."

"It never passed my lips," she promised.

The two men both laughed now, and she pretended to be offended.

The moment was interrupted by Trevor, who called, "Hey, Dad! Look!"

His father went to watch him head the ball to the other boy. Beside Karin, Bruce said not a word. He had gone completely still, his face expressionless.

As if he felt her scrutiny, he let his arm drop from around her shoulders and he turned and walked back toward the others. She looked after him, her heart aching. Trevor hadn't even glanced at Bruce. He'd been too eager to share his pride and delight at his new accomplishment with his father.

She couldn't summon a single word to say that would help.

CHAPTER TWELVE

BRUCE INHALED the scent of Karin's hair, tickling his chin and nose. They'd made love and were still entwined in bed, her head on his chest. He'd been lying here feeling good, but also... He couldn't identify this unease. There was some kind of struggle going on inside him. As if part of him was panicking, even as the rest was feeling happier than he'd known he could be.

"My mother called today," he heard himself say.

Weird. That wasn't even what he'd been thinking about.

She moved, tilting her head so she could see his face, or at least his chin. "Really?"

"Yeah, she does every now and again."

"You made it sound as if you never talked to your parents."

"Never do to my father."

She was quiet for a minute, probably perplexed. "Did she have news?"

"Dad has cancer."

Now Karin pushed back and lifted onto one elbow, studying him with worry. Her corn-silk hair tumbled over her shoulders and arm. "Is it treatable?"

"He's having chemotherapy, but she admitted the prognosis isn't good. Plus, the treatment is making him really sick."

"Does he want to see you?"

Surprised, Bruce said, "God, no! Why would he? This is not a man who's going to discover his kinder, softer self on his deathbed. Trust me."

"But…what about you? How do you feel about knowing he may be dying?"

Therapist speaking, or woman? He guessed, from the concern on her face, that it was the woman asking. She genuinely imagined he'd be broken up about his old man's possible demise.

"Don't give a damn." He examined his own feelings, and realized that he meant it. "I'm not sure what my mother will do without him, though."

What she *should* do was throw a party. In his opinion champagne was in order. But the reality was, she'd have no idea how to function on her own. She'd never been allowed to make decisions.

"Is she close to your brothers and their wives?"

"My next older brother, Dan, the most. He's not as bad as Roger." Which wasn't saying much.

"Would she move up here?"

Bruce shook his head. "She's got the neighborhood. It's her comfort zone. Plus, my brothers and their wives and children are there."

"So you have nieces and nephews?"

"Yeah, I guess. I mean, I've never met them."

He could see her struggling to process these things he'd never told her.

"You really did cut yourself off, didn't you?" she said at last.

"Oh, yeah. And," he warned, afraid she'd feel a mission, "I won't be trying to span the chasm. But Mom…" Uncomfortable, he admitted, "I felt bad. She sounded lost."

Karin continued to watch him in the penetrating way that undoubtedly worked to extract deep dark confessions from her clients. When she made an observation, she kept it neutral. "You love her."

He felt himself twitching. If it wouldn't have been a dead giveaway to her, he'd have sprung from the bed and paced.

"Yeah, sure. Not enough to fly home to hold her hand at my father's bedside, but…yeah."

"Good," she said simply.

"Why good?"

Karin didn't answer, and that weird pressure in his chest of which he'd been aware earlier returned. Or maybe he just noticed it again. After a minute, she sat up and said, "I need the bathroom," swung her feet to the floor and walked out.

He appreciated the view from behind, even as he attempted to pin down his discomfiture. He loved her body: long legs, firm butt that still gave him a couple of handfuls, small waist, tangle of hair. The view was every bit as fine from the front, too, with that gorgeous face and perfect breasts.

Yeah, but a lot of women had great bodies. If there

wasn't a lot more going on, he wouldn't have risked getting involved. Any woman would be getting ideas by now. He was a little startled to realize he wouldn't have liked it if she wasn't starting to envision a future with him.

You want *her to be in love with you?*

He stared up at the ceiling.

Yeah. Yeah, he did.

He should have been surprised to realize the un-thinkable. He didn't want to live without this woman. Without the way she had of looking at him and seeing far more than he'd meant to show. The way she had of understanding and forgiving frailties, of caring passion-ately, of guarding herself.

He had never in his life had this desire to tell another person everything, to share what was bothering him, what shamed him, what pleased him. Now, not a damn thing happened during the day that he didn't immedi-ately think, *I'll tell Karin.*

Dismay punched him. Or maybe shock. *God.* Was this love? Was that what this shaky feeling meant, this sense he had of standing on a crumbling precipice?

Maybe.

He heard her footsteps in the hall and turned his head, waiting to drink in the first sight of her.

Maybe? Who the hell was he kidding?

But would it last? Would it stand up to the crap life threw at everyone?

And maybe the biggest question: Could he give her what she wanted? He hadn't grown up with any kind of role model for ideal husband and dad. Did he have a chance in hell of being the man he suspected she thought he was?

She came into the room, still gloriously naked. If she was anything but utterly composed as she walked toward him, it didn't show.

"Because I'd like to think you do know how to love," she said, as if there'd been no gap between his earlier question and now. "Maybe for my sake, mostly for yours."

Maybe for my sake meant…that she was admitting she loved him?

He could ask. But then, depending on her answer, he'd have to declare himself. Or not. And then… God, then, the crumbling ground beneath his feet would collapse. And he couldn't fly.

So he said, "Yeah, I thought about asking Mom to move up here. She'll say no, but… I might ask."

Karin's smile blossomed, warm and approving. "Might, huh? Heart of stone."

He held out an arm to welcome her. She stretched out beside him, breasts pressed against him, and kissed his jaw, then nibbled on his earlobe.

"Tough guy," she whispered.

"That's me."

It was the last thing he could find voice to say for a while. Which was maybe a good thing, considering his fear of the words he wanted to say.

MONDAY, BRUCE HAD MANAGED to knock off early and pick up Trevor after school, taking him to a community-center playground to play some one-on-one. He needed distraction from his awareness that it was four weeks to the day since Escobar had smashed in his wife's head, killed Julia Lopez and snatched the children.

Four weeks, and the likelihood of Escobar being found receded by the day.

Shaking his head, Bruce dribbled and shot the basketball.

It bounced off the rim, rattling the playground backboard. Trevor sprang to retrieve it.

Hands still extended for the shot, Bruce glowered at the still-quivering rim. "Well, hell."

"You tell me not to swear." Grinning, Trevor dribbled in a circle around him, his feet dancing.

"New shoes," Bruce said, noticing.

"They're cool, aren't they?"

He glanced down to admire. Bruce deftly swiped the ball and swung away, dribbled twice and shot again.

The ball sprang off the rim again. *Clang.*

Trevor cackled, retrieved it again, then drove right past a dumbfounded Bruce and laid it up. The ball slid through the ragged net with barely a whisper.

Bruce shook his head. "Showing me up, are you?"

"I beat Dad at horse yesterday." Trevor gave him a nervous glance. "'Course, he's not as good as you."

"Who is?" Bruce said with mock egoism. He grinned. "Did your dad play high-school ball?"

"Yeah, but he says he wasn't a star or anything."

"You sure he wasn't letting you win?"

Trevor shook his head. "He's out of practice. But it was fun."

"Glad to hear it." Bruce scooped up the ball from where it lay on the asphalt playground and considered how to handle this.

I guess I'm asking you to support my right to be his father.

So little to ask. So much.

"I'm glad he's got time just to hang with you."

"He's been spending a *lot* of time with me," Trevor said with new eagerness, as if given permission to express it. "I heard him on the phone last weekend. Some friend wanted him to go do something. He said, 'I've got my boy living with me now, you know. We have plans.' Only, we didn't really have plans. I mean, not like anything important. We just went to the mall to get me shoes and stuff."

"That's big plans," Bruce said gravely. "You're going to spend that much money you've got to consider it important."

"They cost a bunch." Trevor looked down at his shoes in awe. "I never had *anything* that cost so much before."

Bruce dribbled the ball idly, by instinct. It slapped the asphalt and returned to his hand, the beat rhythmic.

"It sounds like your dad's being good to you."

"He's not anything like I remember." Trevor hesitated. "Could Mom have been wrong about him?"

Bruce held a lightning internal debate, then chose honesty. "No. You remember them fighting, right? Your dad really drunk. Your mom's face all swollen and bruised."

"Both her eyes were black this one time." Trevor's

face screwed up with the remembering. His voice was slow, reluctant. He didn't want this amazing father he had now to be the same man who'd hurt his mother. "So how come he's so nice now?"

Bruce finally palmed the basketball and held it under his arm. "People can change. Mostly, though, I imagine his drinking was the problem. Some people don't handle alcohol very well. It lowers your inhibitions." Noting Trevor's confusion, he said, "When you're drunk, you act on what you're feeling. You're real happy, or real depressed, or real angry. So a drunk person tends to be jovial, or weepy, or violent. From what your mother told me, your dad tended to be angry and violent."

Trevor nodded.

"And then, it may be that your mother and father were having problems that weren't all one-sided. You know she used drugs."

There was a discernible pause before Trevor gave a short, unhappy nod.

"Your dad wasn't always happy about that. And the stuff she was using changed *her* personality, so she probably said and did things she wouldn't have otherwise." And that was enough on that subject, Bruce decided, watching the boy's face. "The good part is, your mother took action and asked him to leave. And your dad loved you enough to realize he had to deal with his problems."

"Is that why he quit drinking? Me?"

"That's what he says. And I don't know any reason not to believe him. Do you?"

A sharp breeze was coming off the sound. Trevor shivered. "No."

"It might be that now you're seeing the man your father would have been if he had never started drinking," Bruce said. "Or maybe not. Maybe he's a better man *because* he feels bad about those years. We learn from our mistakes."

Trevor was silent again for a minute. He appeared very young at this moment, skinny and vulnerable, the boy who'd been victimized every day at the bus stop, who'd huddled in an empty apartment scraping for enough to eat while he waited for his mother to come home.

Bruce's chest hurt suddenly, and he knew he loved this kid. Knew he'd have been a good father if he had had the guts to take him home.

What hurt now was realizing his insight was way too late out of the starting gate. Trevor's biological father was doing a good job, too, and he loved Trevor. Like he'd said, he had a right.

"I miss Mom sometimes," Trevor said in a small voice.

"Of course you do." Bruce stepped forward and wrapped an arm around the boy.

For a moment, he leaned against Bruce. Then, with a sniff, he straightened. "I keep thinking she wouldn't like me being with Dad."

So that was what was bothering him. He thought he was betraying his mom by loving his father.

Bruce shook his head. "One thing you've got to remember is that way back, when they first met and got married and decided to have you, she loved him. What she got to hating was the guy who drank too much and was mad all the time. Letting go of that hate was hard. She had trouble believing your dad had really changed. But I think she'd be really glad to know he actually has, and that you're safe and loved. She loved you more than anything herself, and she'd want whatever is best for you."

Trevor swiped at his face and half turned away, embarrassed to be caught crying. "She's dead, isn't she?" he mumbled.

"I suspect so." Or caught in the purgatory between life and death that was a crack addict's final months. "She wouldn't have stayed away otherwise."

The twelve-year-old nodded, his face bleak but his expression showing that he was also comforted by his faith that nothing but death would have made his mother abandon him.

"You'll keep coming to see me, right?" he asked.

Bruce smiled and squeezed his shoulder, hiding his own grief. Trevor wouldn't need him for much longer. "Are you kidding? Of course I will."

"Okay," the boy said, relaxing at the reassurance, the promise that Bruce wouldn't let go until he was ready.

"You hungry?"

"Yeah!"

They started walking toward the car, the ball still tucked under Bruce's arm. "Pizza?"

Trevor cast him a scornful look. "We always have pizza."

"You might've just had it."

"I never get tired of pizza. It's my favorite food.

Except, Dad makes really great tacos. He doesn't say I have to put tomatoes or anything on them. I like to just have the meat and cheese and sour cream. But he doesn't buy those hard tortillas, like Mom did."

"The ones that are always stale."

"Yeah! Dad gets these corn ones that are fresh from some little store, and he heats them up, and then he…"

Bruce listened to him rhapsodize about his father's culinary genius, followed by his father's exemplary taste in movies and clothes and pretty much everything else, and felt that ache under his own breastbone.

This was the crummy part of loving someone: the having to let go.

TUESDAY, BRUCE AND KARIN had lunch, as they'd taken to doing regularly at one of the half-dozen cafés near A Woman's Hand. They were sitting at a sidewalk table under a green, leafy tree, talking about the latest imbroglio involving the police chief and the city council, when his cell phone rang.

He glanced at the screen—253 area code, meaning south of Seattle down through Tacoma. He didn't recognize the number, but excused himself and answered.

"Detective Walker."

The spate of apologetic Spanish required him to shift gears.

"Señora Sanchez?" For a moment he didn't recognize the name. Then it clicked. Vicente Sanchez, the owner of the vehicle when Bruce ran the license plates. This was the woman from the Kent grocery store, the one who'd showed a flicker of recognition when she saw the photo on his flyer.

"I wasn't sure," she was telling him. "I asked my sister to go look at the picture, too, because she is better with faces than I am. She says the tall man in your picture is Carlos Jimenez."

Satisfaction filled him. So, even though Carlos had used a fake last name at the lumberyard, he'd stuck with his given name. People on the run often did.

Karin was watching him, her gaze arrested by his expression.

"And how do you know this Carlos Jimenez?" he asked.

Carlos lived in a trailer a couple of miles from them, Señora Sanchez informed him. Bruce gathered from her disdain that his was a run-down place, not that nice, perhaps trashy. She'd heard he was away, that he'd worked the strawberry fields earlier and might be picking blueberries down in Oregon now. She only knew him a little—which was why she hadn't been sure that day.

"Can you tell me how to find Señor Jimenez's place?" He kept his voice easy. "Perhaps he's there after all."

"I asked other people," Señora Sanchez said. "They say someone else is living there right now. A man who isn't very friendly."

He sat up, his elbow jostling his coffee cup. Karin snatched it before it could go over. Bruce hardly noticed.

"Have children been seen there, too? Did this person notice?"

"She thought she saw a little girl in the window. When she told me that, I decided I should tell you. For poor Señora Escobar's sake."

"You did the right thing," he reassured her. "If the man isn't Roberto Escobar, there's no harm done. Like I told you, I don't care about papers."

After further nudging on his part, she told him where Jimenez's shabby trailer was. He thanked her several times, and was finally able to end the call.

Karin had been waiting, lips parted. "You learned something."

"The woman saw my flyer and recognized Roberto's friend. But the friend is away, and someone is staying at his trailer."

"You think it's Roberto."

"Don't get too excited," he warned her. "False leads are a hell of a lot more common than good ones."

"But *you're* excited," she observed.

She knew him too well.

"I've got a feeling," Bruce admitted. "But my gut's been wrong before. I'll check out the place this afternoon."

"Will you call me? Immediately? I want to be with Lenora if you find them."

"I promise," he said. He would have anyway. She'd been with him every step of the way on this one. She deserved no less.

They'd both lost interest in lingering. He paid and they walked back to the clinic, where they parted. Using his cell phone, Bruce let Molly know where he was going.

Señora Sanchez's directions took him to a rural part of the Auburn Valley. He'd never been in this particular area before, and was a little surprised at how run-down most of the houses were. The prosperity that had sent real-estate values skyrocketing in most of King County hadn't reached this far south of the city yet. To each side of the road, fences sagged, yards were filled with disemboweled cars and trucks set up on cinder blocks, the paint on houses peeled, and mailboxes were dented and listing on semirotted posts.

He passed the Sanchez home, and noted that although it was modest, this yard was tidy and someone had encased the mailbox in a steel barrel to protect it from the baseball bats teenage vandals liked to use when cruising rural roads.

Go one mile farther, she'd instructed him, and turn at the purple house. Which was indeed an eye-popping purple. The owners were also fond of plastic garden decor, from a wishing well to multiple deer, rabbit and gnome statues.

A quarter of a mile farther, he found the dirt road that she'd described to the left. A row of mailboxes at the corner told him that there were eight inhabited properties down this road. He could drive partway.

These houses and trailers were scattered far apart, each set on an acre or more. A couple had pastures containing spavined horses or a few goats. A cloud of dust plumed behind his car, although he drove slowly. He could see the dead end of the road ahead when he made the decision to pull to a wide bit of shoulder and walk.

Feeling conspicuous, he hoped like hell no one—
and especially Roberto Escobar—happened to drive
by right now. Maybe he should have left his car out at
the main road.

Yeah, and then he'd have had to walk farther. No one
who spotted him would mistake him for anything but a
cop.

Three driveways split at the end of the road.
Jimenez's was the one that led to the left. Bruce took
advantage of a stand of scraggly alder trees and vine
maples and left the gravel road, trespassing over
someone's land. He moved slowly between the narrow
trees, carefully, pausing to listen. The hair on the back
of his neck had begun to prickle. He kept having flash-
backs to army reconnaissance missions.

On the edge of the small woods, he found a towering
mass of blackberries, thorny and impassable. Sucking
his hand and swearing, he backtracked until he found
an opening that allowed him to look across a grassy field
studded with more, leggier blackberry vines to the
single-wide mobile home Señora Sanchez had described. Indeed, it appeared barely habitable, set up on
blocks, like the rusting hulks of cars and trucks that also
made the property unsightly.

From here, he couldn't see whether any vehicle that
still had wheels was parked beside the trailer. He wished
he routinely carried binoculars. He set his phone to vibrate
rather than ring. Then, using the cover provided by the
derelicts in the yard, Bruce bent low and trotted through
the grass, crouching finally behind an ancient tractor.

He inched to peer around it, and gave a feral grin when he saw the dented blue Buick. Goddamn. Escobar *was* here. He hoped like hell the children were, as well.

Bruce settled in for what might be a long wait. He had plenty of practice at stakeouts. He let his mind free-float while he crouched, scarcely blinking as he watched the trailer. He remembered Lenora, frail and wary, in that first self-defense workshop, then the sight of her crumpled body in the parking lot. Her still figure in the hospital bed, chest rising and falling but no other sign of life. Karin sitting beside the bed, talking about gardening and mothers and the happenings outside the walls of the hospital, amused and vibrant and thoughtful. Most of all, he envisioned Lenora Escobar once she'd awakened, her huge, haunted, dark eyes brimming with tears.

Oh, yeah. He could sit here for the next two days if he had to.

But it wasn't more than an hour later that he heard a child crying, then a man's angry voice, too muffled for words to be distinguishable. Another voice—a girl's? It, too, rose to a wail. A door slammed. Something crashed inside, and the first sobs abruptly cut off. The second, shriller, ones hung in the air an instant longer, like an echo, then fell silent, as well.

Bruce saw a shadow move inside, a figure passing back and forth in front of one of the windows. The pace seemed quick and agitated.

Not enjoying single parenthood, Roberto?

Time passed. Bruce waited. At last, the front door—

or was it the only exit? he'd have to check—opened. A man stood on the top step, scanning the yard, his gaze narrowed and suspicious. Had a neighbor called, mentioning the strange vehicle parked beside the road?

But after a moment Roberto pulled a pack of cigarettes from his shirt pocket and lit up. Relaxing infinitesimally, Bruce realized suspicion was Roberto Escobar's constant companion these days.

"Papa?" a small voice called from the open door behind him.

He turned and snarled something, then swung back to face the yard. The child didn't ask again.

Movement at one of the windows caught Bruce's attention. A child's face appeared. As Señora Sanchez's friend had said, a little girl's. She must be standing on something to peek out. In that glimpse, Bruce read desolation.

Anna Escobar, at least, still lived. Bruce guessed the first cry must have been the little boy's. From the sequence of cries, he thought Anna must be doing a nearly-five-year-old's best to protect her younger brother, or at least to deflect their father's rage. She had learned, perhaps, from watching her mother.

At last Roberto went back inside. Eyes on the single-wide, Bruce pulled out his cell phone and made the calls that would bring out a SWAT team. He faded back to the stand of trees and made his way in a large circle around the trailer, which had no other door. Then he walked rapidly to his car. Not until he was out on the main road and had chosen a driveway that looked rarely used, where he could park and watch unseen for the

Buick in case Roberto decided to make a run to the grocery store, did he dial his phone again.

"I found them," he told Karin.

CHAPTER THIRTEEN

BRUCE HAD MADE the decision to move a team into place around the perimeter of the single-wide mobile home, but otherwise to wait until Roberto emerged to go to the store or do another errand. Hell, if he'd just take a few steps from the front door while having his smoke they might be able to bring him down. Bruce wanted him to be separated from the children when they attempted to make the arrest. A man as cold-blooded and egocentric as he was wouldn't hesitate to use the children to evade capture.

One by one, black-suited SWAT-team members slipped across the field and took up their stances behind the hulks of cars, trucks and tractors that studded the yard. A couple eased up to the single-wide itself, where they flattened themselves against the exterior walls so they couldn't be seen through the windows.

They'd considered trying to get in through one of the windows to the children, perhaps passing them through, but given the children's ages, the consensus was that they couldn't be trusted not to cry out. And the windows were small. Even an adult Molly's size, say, would have a hell of a time squeezing in. It wasn't going to happen without alerting Escobar, whose frequent, restless appearances at the front door suggested that he was hypervigilant.

A couple of snipers were in place, as well, and Bruce knew they were itching to take that shot, but until Escobar threatened one of the kids, killing him wasn't justified.

The girl's face appeared a couple more times. Bruce, sitting behind a pickup truck that had no axles or wheels, wondered what she was looking for.

The afternoon and early evening passed with no indication Roberto had any intention of going anywhere. Every cop in hiding tensed when he walked out once. Were they going to have a go? But, whatever he'd planned, he wheeled and went inside.

Back in the trees, they started holding a discussion. Did they camp out here all night? Hope for a chance tomorrow? Bruce didn't like the odds in a confrontation.

Bruce talked to Karin and Lenora a couple of times as the excruciating hours crawled by. He knew that Lenora's anguish must be a thousand times his own.

The decision of whether or not to wait was snatched out of his hands.

Bruce was sitting with his back to the rusting door of his chosen cover, when he heard a crash followed by the scream of tortured metal, a shout and an even louder crash. It sounded like a goddamn car accident, right there in the yard.

Growling an obscenity, he rose to a crouch.

One of the cars had fallen off its blocks. A cop lay half beneath. He was trying to sit up, but was pinned.

His face was twisted in agony, his teeth gritted. As if not screaming now would make any difference.

The door to the trailer snapped open. Roberto stared across the yard, let out a single expletive and disappeared within.

Bruce's earbud crackled. "What do we do? What do we do?" asked a couple of difference voices.

"The damn thing fell right on Fulton's *legs,*" someone else said.

A second SWAT-team member was now crouched beside him. Someone else ran forward, and the two cops strained to lift the rusting heap to free their colleague.

The door to the mobile home opened again, and Roberto reappeared, his little girl in his arms and the barrel of a handgun pressed to her head. Most of his body was obscured by the door and by her. He wasn't taking any chances.

"Show yourselves!" he yelled in Spanish. "Show yourselves now!"

"Not everyone," Bruce murmured, then stood, holding his hands up.

Four other officers stood, as well, all doing the same. *See? We're harmless.*

"I'll kill her!" Roberto Escobar's face was that of a madman. Sweat dripped from him, and his eyes were wild. When Anna kept struggling, his arm snapped tight abruptly, viciously. She retched. "If you try to come in, I will shoot you, and I will kill them both."

Still holding the gun on his own daughter, he backed inside and yanked the door shut behind him.

More men ran forward to lift the car, finally dragging Fulton out.

A window scraped open. Their heads lifted. The barrel of a rifle slid into sight, and they all flung themselves to each side as it cracked. Bullets banged off the metal.

Men crawled, belly to the ground, a couple dragging their injured officer. Dirt and grass spat into the air when shots hit nearby. Then the barrel disappeared and the window closed.

Bruce began to swear again. This was his worst nightmare. Even Escobar hadn't had any idea how to get out of this. A man of limited education and experience, born paranoid—what was he going to ask for? A helicopter to carry him away? A Hummer?

No. Escobar knew he was trapped, knew they wouldn't, couldn't, let him go. Another man might have meditated, realized he was done and released his children. Maybe killed himself, but not the kids. Roberto would *want* to kill them, especially if he'd found out his wife had survived. Right this second, he'd be dreaming up an ugly, newsworthy end.

Would he do it right away? Did they have time?

A calm voice spoke at his side. "Did we get a phone number?"

Jerry Gullick, one of the top negotiators in the Northwest.

Bruce shook his head. "Phone company says there isn't one in there."

"I've got my bullhorn." He brandished it.

"I doubt he'll talk," Bruce said grimly. "But do your best."

They'd discussed earlier, if this moment came, what leverage Gullick might have with Roberto. They all knew that Lenora might be his one weakness. Bruce hated the idea of playing that card. Roberto wouldn't be persuaded by his wife; he'd want her here only so he could take pleasure in knowing she was watching as he murdered Anna and Enrico.

"Roberto," the negotiator called, stepping into sight. "There is no way out. Let's talk. Open a window so you can hear me and I can hear you."

Bruce dropped back for a consultation.

"We could lob in a canister of gas," someone suggested.

A captain shook his head. "He'd hear the window breaking. Even a couple seconds' warning is too much."

"And do we know the effect on a baby?" asked Bruce.

"They're his own *children*." More incredulity from a lieutenant.

Bruce tried to remember what it was that the uncle had said about Escobar.

He thought it was his right. As if he were God inside his own house.

Bruce said flatly, "He's incapable of loving them. They're *his*. A statement."

If a man can't be king in his own castle…

Not comparable, Bruce thought. His father, whatever his sins, would have run into a burning building to save one of his sons. He was a son of a bitch who believed he had a right to indulge his temper, but he wasn't a monster.

Not like Roberto Escobar.

Bruce left the huddle of men, walked a few feet and turned his back. He flipped open his cell phone.

Karin was waiting at the hospital with Lenora. She answered on the first ring.

"We screwed up," Bruce told her bluntly.

Her breath hissed in.

"The kids are fine still. I think they're fine," he added conscientiously, not wanting to lie. He told her about the car collapsing from its cinder blocks, presumably because someone had been leaning against it without realizing it was precariously balanced. The injured officer, the shots, Escobar's appearance with a gun to his daughter's head, the controlled hysteria.

"Our negotiator's talking to him right now, but Escobar isn't answering."

"Do you need me to bring Lenora?"

God. He wanted to say no, keep her far, far away. But he knew she was their only hope of luring Escobar out. And he knew, as well, that she wouldn't hesitate to sacrifice herself for the sake of her children.

He hated to think she might have to, but right this minute he didn't have any other ideas.

"Yeah. I'm sending someone to pick you up. You need to get here quick."

Karin said only, calmly, "We're ready."

He made another call, getting a uniform to fetch them and haul ass down here.

After grabbing a pair of binoculars, he studied the mobile home again. It was a relic of the sixties, at his guess; metal siding, once white, was scabbed with rust and curled up at the seams. He could imagine the floors were rotting. They could get under it, see if there was an easy place to punch up.

Same problem as going in the window. Short of teleporting, there was no way in without giving warning.

When he returned to Gullick's side, the negotiator murmured, "He cracked a window. He's listening."

"Good. What are you promising?"

"I'm not promising. I'm asking him what we can do. I'm reminding him that his children depend on him for protection, that their papa is a great man to them."

"Uh-huh."

Gullick returned to the bullhorn, his voice as magic as the highest paid DJ's, smooth and soothing. Right now, he was Escobar's best friend, his salvation. Thank God he spoke fluent Spanish.

Maybe instead of lobbing a gas canister in a window, they could quietly pop a hole in the floor. Insert it that way.

Bruce remembered the photo taken at Christmas of little Anna and Enrico and cursed under his breath.

The front door opened again, just a crack. Anna, held in her father's arms, appeared. He was no more than a dark shadow behind her.

Through the crack he shouted, "I will kill one of the children if you don't go away. You have five minutes." The door snapped shut again.

Swearing, Bruce grabbed the bullhorn. "Roberto, your wife is on her way. She wants to talk to you. We can't let her come if we aren't here to protect her."

There was a pause. Then, through the window, he called, "If she wants to talk, she must walk up to the steps alone. No one with her."

"No. You talk from this distance."

Silence.

"Do I have your promise to wait for her? You won't hurt Anna or Enrico?"

His voice, disembodied and less angry than earlier, was more disturbing devoid of rage. "When she comes." The window slid shut.

Behind him, Bruce heard someone say, "What the hell does *that* mean?"

But they all knew. Roberto wanted his wife to suffer.

This wait was more agonizing than all the previous hours put together. Nothing and no one could be seen moving inside the single-wide. Out here, every idea presented was shot down as fast.

"Goddamn tin can," Bruce's father used to call mobile homes. In this case, he was right. The windows were tiny, the door next to impossible to break down, the metal siding as good as a soup can at protecting its contents. Bruce tried to picture what Roberto was doing inside. Had he forced the children to lie down? Were they huddled in a corner? Why was neither crying? Were they that terrified of their father, even at their tender age? Or was Enrico already dead?

Bruce swore aloud, earning him a sidelong look from Gullick and from Marston, his captain. Neither commented.

The squad car carrying the two women pulled

partway up the dirt driveway before rolling to a stop. Why not? Roberto knew his wife was coming. Surprise wasn't a realistic goal here.

The two got out and walked to Bruce, Karin half supporting Lenora, who moved slowly and with difficulty. Her face was as white as those damn hospital sheets, the underlying bones stark without the softening effect of hair. Her eyes, despairing, dominated it.

Bruce tore his gaze away long enough to meet Karin's. She looked little better than Lenora. He hated seeing her so afraid, so aware that she was helpless to change what was to come.

"I'm sorry," he said, taking Lenora's hand. "It shouldn't have ended up like this."

"Perhaps it had to." The small Hispanic woman gave a shrug. Her voice was soft and somehow fatalistic. "It's me he wants to hurt."

Releasing her hand, he said, "I thought we could get the children out of this."

"I will offer myself." Despite the determination in her tone, her glance at the mobile home betrayed her terror. "But he must let Anna and Enrico go. Do you think he'll do that?"

"We want him to *think* he'll get you in exchange. We can't let him get his hands on you."

She bit her lip so hard blood smeared it, "I won't risk them. Only they matter. He will know if you try to trick him." She hesitated. "Have you seen them?"

"Only Anna," he admitted. "Earlier, I thought I heard two children crying, but that was hours ago."

Tears welled in her eyes, but she brushed impatiently at them. "He knows I'm here now."

"Yes."

If Roberto was looking out the window, what did he feel? Was he angry that his wife still lived? Did he feel even a pang of regret, perhaps remember slowly unbraiding her glossy dark hair, back when it hung nearly to her waist and when she would have gazed up at him trustingly?

Bruce issued instructions to her without any expectation they could be followed. Eyes trained on his face, she nodded.

Finally, Gullick asked, "Are we ready?"

Ready? Realistically, they weren't going to be tricking Roberto Escobar. They had only the hope of sacrificing this brave woman for the two young children she loved so much that she faced death without hesitation.

Inside, Bruce raged, but he gave a curt nod.

Gullick lifted the bullhorn. "Roberto, Lenora is here."

The front door opened. They all waited, breathless, none more than Lenora, who pressed her hand to her breast as if to still her heart. Karin held her closer, if possible.

Again, it was Anna he held up. Even from this distance, they could all see that one side of her face was bruised and swollen. Her eyes found her mother, and her mouth formed the silent, desperate cry *Mama.* Lenora's breath hissed in. Bruce fought to hold on to his cool.

"If you don't want to watch her die, you will come by yourself to the door."

"We told you she'd talk from this distance," the negotiator said.

"Then I'll kill Anna right now."

He must have rammed the barrel tighter against his daughter's head. Her eyes widened and she began to struggle.

"No!" Lenora called, and wrenched herself free from Karin's encircling arm. "I'll come if you will let Anna and Enrico both go."

"You lie!" he bellowed.

"No." She walked forward a few steps.

Bruce's every instinct was to snatch her back. It took everything he had in him to let her do what she must.

"Where is Enrico?" she asked. "Bring him out. I want to see him."

After a moment, the little girl was pulled back from the opening. A toddler was lifted instead. He wore no diaper, only a T-shirt. His face was soaked with tears that must have been shed silently, an extraordinary feat for a child that age.

Lenora's whole body jerked. "Let them walk out to meet me." Her voice was now eerily calm. "You can shoot them if I don't keep coming."

The silence was absolute. They all knew he might pull the trigger right now, throw the boy's body out for his horrified wife to see. That might be all he wanted, to kill their children in front of her, then himself. To leave her shattered.

Bruce reached out and gripped Karin's hand. She held on as tightly, her fear palpable in the connection.

After a moment, the door opened wider, just enough to allow the little girl to slip out.

She wore a dress; a pretty one, red, with white lace and a puffy skirt below which her legs were skinny and bare. That dress was so incongruous it struck a bizarre note. She raced to her mother, her hair flying behind her, tears streaming down her face now.

Lenora ran forward to meet her and fell to her knees. Their bodies met, and the weeping little girl vanished in her mother's enfolding arms. She held her and rocked her for a moment that was heartbreakingly brief, then lifted her head and said clearly, "Now Enrico."

"I want you closer first."

She bowed her head and spoke to the little girl. Lenora's hands lifted and smoothed her child's hair lovingly, lingeringly. Anna might never know that touch again, but she wouldn't forget it. Then Lenora stood, looked toward Karin and gave her daughter a gentle push.

Karin dropped Bruce's hand and stepped forward, kneeling with her arms out. The girl came to her, but with many backward glances. Once, she stumbled and fell. Finally, she let Karin in turn enfold her, but swiveled in her arms to stare yearningly back at her mother.

Steadily, Lenora walked forward. She wasn't five feet from the rickety steps when Enrico emerged. He scrambled down them on his short legs and raced in turn to his mother. Again, she crouched and held him. Not a single cop watching could tear his gaze from the reunion.

Finally, she sent him on his way, as well. He might not have been willing had he not had his sister in his sights. He ran to her, and the two seemed to meld, so closely did they cling.

Without a backward glance, Lenora climbed the steps. She never glanced toward the cops flattened against the wall, one perhaps ten feet to her left, another at the corner.

"Do you have a shot?" Marston was demanding. "Goddamn it, do you have a shot?"

In their headsets, they heard the sniper in the best position saying urgently, "I can't make him out. Damn it, she's in the way. Now she's in the way."

This was the moment for her to fling herself to one side. Roberto would have a shot, but only one. Instead, his arm snaked out and snatched her inside. She seemed to go meekly, her head bent. Incredulous, Bruce realized she'd never intended to avoid her fate.

But the door didn't shut. Something was happening inside. A scuffle, a clatter. A howl of rage.

The two closest SWAT-team members flung themselves up the steps. Bruce was running before his brain ordered, *Move!* What was happening? Why no shot?

It was over by the time he threw himself up the steps and inside. Roberto Escobar was facedown on the floor, writhing, cuffs being snapped on his wrists. He was screaming obscenities.

Lenora had backed away, hand to her mouth, staring at him. Huge shudders shook her. Bruce assessed the scene with a lightning glance. The handgun lay ten feet away, as if it had been kicked across the filthy, carpeted floor.

He took her in his arms, turning her away from the monster who had fathered her children and would have killed them rather than let her leave him. "What happened?" Bruce asked over her head.

One of the cops shook his head. "Somehow she brought him down. He was on the floor when I got in the door."

Lenora pushed away from Bruce and swung around to stare venomously at the man being hauled to his feet. "He thought I couldn't fight back. But somehow I knew what I should do. I chopped, like this—" she demonstrated a vicious snap of her hand "—and the gun fell to the ground. And then I kneed him, there."

Bruce had never in his life seen a look like the one Roberto Escobar gave his wife over his shoulder as he was shoved out the door. Baffled hatred and incredulity.

She was right. It had never occurred to him that she would fight back.

Bruce found himself grinning. Maybe it was inappropriate. This minute, he didn't care.

"It was the self-defense workshop," he realized. "We talked about those things. A chop of the hand and run. And where a man's most vulnerable."

"That," she said with an odd primness, "I already knew." Then, suddenly, her eyes filled with tears. "Anna! Enrico!"

She flew out the door and down the steps, then ran, lurching, across the field, passing her husband now surrounded by half a dozen cops. Karin let the kids go and they raced to their mother, both crying, "Mama, Mama, Mama!" the whole way.

Bruce watched both them and Karin, standing directly behind them. Once again, her fingers were pressed to her mouth, but now tears streamed down her face, too. She lifted her gaze to meet Bruce's, and hers was filled with joy so transcendent, he felt it like a blow.

No, like a caress.

I can't live without her.

And then, without the slightest difficulty, he thought, *I love her.*

THE CHILDREN WERE SKINNY and dirty and traumatized. Both stuck to their mother like leeches. Bruce guessed it would be several years before they would be pried loose for any length of time. But Lenora held them with extraordinary tenderness, speaking softly, pressing kisses to their cheeks and the tops of their heads. It was as if no one else existed.

Bruce felt something like envy. He had never seriously considered having children of his own before. But watching Lenora with her two children, watching Karin hovering over them, he felt like an idiot. Yeah, of course he was in love. And he couldn't imagine anything better than to have kids with her.

He wanted to be alone with her. Right now. He wanted to drag her into his arms and kiss her. He wanted to make passionate love to her, before or after he went down on bended knee and asked her to marry him.

Adrenaline kept pumping through him. His chest felt bruised, after hours of despair and the heart-wrenching sight of a mother reassuring her young children and then saying goodbye to them, in a way they might not have recognized but that every adult had. How had he gotten to his age *without* seeing how powerful love could be?

Of course, it was hours before he had a chance to exchange more than a few words with Karin.

Lenora and the kids went to the hospital, where her family enveloped them. Bruce's last sight of Roberto for the night was in the back of a squad car, his face a blur as he stared with dark, angry eyes.

Karin finally went home, but not before pausing at Bruce's side and saying, "Will you come when you can?"

"Yeah." He touched her face. Didn't trust himself to kiss her. He might not be able to stop.

He didn't get away for hours.

It was just after two in the morning when he knocked on her door. The porch light was on, and at least one lamp in the living room. Nonetheless, he barely tapped, in case she'd fallen asleep.

The door opened and she stepped forward as he did the same. His arms closed convulsively around her. For a moment he just held her. Why did he feel this way? he wondered. Neither of them had had a near-death experience today, or even been in danger. But he felt as if they had, as if they needed to grab and hold on to each other.

Karin pulled back. "Did you *see* her? Wasn't she amazing?"

"Yeah." His voice was rough. "She was amazing."

"You taught her to do that."

"She doesn't remember the class."

"But somehow she did. When she needed to."

Okay, damn it, that did feel good. He'd done something worthwhile. Knowing that helped a little, because his heart hadn't been the only thing bruised today. His ego had been, too. He'd be rethinking every damn decision he'd made for a long time to come. They'd been a blink of the eye from tragedy today, and he would have blamed himself. In the end, he hadn't been able to help Lenora. She'd had to rescue herself. The cop in him didn't like knowing that, even as the man marveled at her extraordinary courage.

"We're standing here for the whole world to see." Karin suddenly sounded self-conscious. She hugged herself and stepped back. Probably she'd just remembered that she wore only a camisole with spaghetti straps and a pair of low-slung pants that looked like sweats but thinner. Yoga pants, maybe. Her nipples showed through the thin knit fabric of the top, clear enough that he hardened at the sight. "Will you stay tonight?"

"Yeah." Gruff again. "I'll stay."

"Good." Her teeth worried her lip. "I think I need you."

"I need you, too."

Her smile warmed. "I'm glad." She shut the door behind him and turned the dead bolt, then moved naturally into his arms again.

The opening was perfect. Bruce suffered a momentary hitch. It reminded him of having to speak for the first time in a foreign language to a group of native speakers. You felt as if you were making an ass of yourself.

So? Be an ass.

Looking down into her face, glowing up at him, he took the leap. "I love you."

Her entire body went still. The smile vanished. Only her eyes were vividly, intensely alive, searching his. "You mean that?" she whispered.

"Yeah." He slid a hand around the back of her neck, reveling in the silk of her skin, the tension and strength and fragility that made up a woman who'd captivated him from the beginning. "I mean it."

"Oh." It was as much a sigh as an exclamation. "I love you, too. You know that, don't you?"

He hadn't expected to feel as if his heart had just been cleaved in half. Excruciating, and weirdly pleasurable. His heart would never be whole again. He imagined himself handing her a chunk of it, bloody and still beating, the wound in his chest open.

Bruce cleared his throat. "I…hoped." With his free hand, he brushed hair back from her forehead, loving the curve of it. "I think, today…" Why was this so hard to say? "We saw love. A different kind, but…indomitable." Not a word he could ever remember using, but it seemed right. "I thought, if he'd had that gun to your head…"

"You would have done anything."

He nodded. "Meeting you changed me."

She actually laughed, a soft sound, and shook her head. "You've always had the capacity to love someone. You do love Trevor."

"I want kids." The words seemed torn from him. "I want you."

Her lips parted in surprise.

"Will you marry me?"

She gave a cry and rose on tiptoe to press her mouth against his. The kiss was long and sweet, shared wonder more than physical hunger, although he felt that, too.

"Yes," Karin murmured against his mouth. "Oh, yes."

"Cops make lousy husbands."

"But you'll understand when I'm immersed in some poor woman's horror, or I have nightmares about a ten-year-old who's been raped by her grandpa."

Yeah, he'd understand. She'd get what he did, too. She was that woman in a million who'd be able to *handle* marriage to a cop.

"I love you," he said again, as if those three simple words summed up every one of the thousand emotions that swelled in his chest.

The amazing thing was, they did. And they got easier to say, too.

Tears sparkled on her lashes, and she murmured, "Now, make love to me."

That part, he'd already learned to do. He and she—they'd never just had sex, he realized sometime later, as he touched her and was touched, as they alternated passion and tenderness. They'd always made love.

Maybe she was right. He hadn't needed therapy to alter some vital part of him so he was able to feel love.

He'd just needed Karin.

* * * * *

THOROUGHBRED LEGACY
The stakes are high when it comes to love,
horse racing, family secrets
and broken promises.

A new exciting Harlequin continuity series
coming soon!
Led by New York Times
bestselling author Elizabeth Bevarly
FLIRTING WITH TROUBLE

Here's a preview!

THE DOOR CLOSED behind them, throwing them into darkness and leaving them utterly alone. And the next thing Daniel knew, he heard himself saying, "Marnie, I'm sorry about the way things turned out in Del Mar."

She said nothing at first, only strode across the room and stared out the window beside him. Although he couldn't see her well in the darkness—he still hadn't switched on a light…but then, neither had she—he imagined her expression was a little preoccupied, a little anxious, a little confused.

Finally, very softly, she said, "Are you?"

He nodded, then, worried she wouldn't be able to see the gesture, added, "Yeah. I am. I should have said goodbye to you."

"Yes, you should have."

Actually, he thought, there were a lot of things he should have done in Del Mar. He'd had *a lot* riding on the Pacific Classic, and even more on his entry, Little Joe, but after meeting Marnie, the Pacific Classic had been the last thing on Daniel's mind. His loss at Del Mar had pretty much ended his career before it had even begun, and he'd had to start all over again, rebuilding from nothing.

He simply had not then and did not now have room in his life for a woman as potent as Marnie Roberts. He was a horseman first and foremost. From the time he was a schoolboy, he'd known what he wanted to do with his life—be the best possible trainer he could be.

He had to make sure Marnie understood—and he understood, too—why things had ended the way they had eight years ago. He just wished he could find the words to do that. Hell, he wished he could find the *thoughts* to do that.

"You made me forget things, Marnie, things that I really needed to remember. And that scared the hell out of me. Little Joe should have won the Classic. He was by far the best horse entered in that race. But I didn't give him the attention he needed and deserved that week, because all I could think about was you. Hell, when I woke up that morning all I wanted to do was lie there and look at you, and then wake you up and make love to you again. If I hadn't left when I did—the way I did—I might still be lying there in that bed with you, thinking about nothing else."

"And would that be so terrible?" she asked.

"Of course not," he told her. "But that wasn't why I was in Del Mar," he repeated. "I was in Del Mar to win a race. That was my job. And my work was the most important thing to me."

She said nothing for a moment, only studied his face in the darkness as if looking for the answer to a very important question. Finally she asked, "And what's the most important thing to you now, Daniel?"

Wasn't the answer to that obvious? "My work," he answered automatically.

She nodded slowly. "Of course," she said softly. "That is, after all, what you do best."

Her comment, too, puzzled him. She made it sound as if being good at what he did was a bad thing.

She bit her lip thoughtfully, her eyes fixed on his, glimmering in the scant moonlight that was filtering through the window. And damned if Daniel didn't find himself wanting to pull her into his arms and kiss her. But as much as it might have felt as if no time had passed since Del Mar, there were eight years between now and then. And eight years was a long time in the best of circumstances. For Daniel and Marnie, it was virtually a lifetime.

So Daniel turned and started for the door, then halted. He couldn't just walk away and leave things as they were, unsettled. He'd done that eight years ago and regretted it.

"It *was* good to see you again, Marnie," he said softly. And since he was being honest, he added, "I hope we see each other again."

She didn't say anything in response, only stood silhouetted against the window with her arms wrapped around her in a way that made him wonder whether she was doing it because she was cold, or if she just needed something—someone—to hold on to. In either case, Daniel understood. There was an emptiness clinging to him that he suspected would be there for a long time.

* * * * *

THOROUGHBRED LEGACY
coming soon wherever books are sold!

Thoroughbred Legacy

Launching in June 2008

A dramatic new 12-book continuity that embodies the American Dream.

Meet the Prestons, owners of Quest Stables, a successful horse-racing and breeding empire. But the lives, loves and reputations of this hardworking family are put at risk when a breeding scandal unfolds.

Flirting with Trouble

by New York Times bestselling author

ELIZABETH BEVARLY

Eight years ago, publicist Marnie Roberts spent seven days of bliss with Australian horse trainer Daniel Whittleson. But just as quickly, he disappeared. Now Marnie is heading to Australia to finally confront the man she's never been able to forget.

The stakes are high when it comes to love, horse racing, family secrets and broken promises.

A new exciting Harlequin continuity series coming soon!

HT38984R

REQUEST YOUR FREE BOOKS!

2 FREE NOVELS PLUS 2 FREE GIFTS!

HARLEQUIN®

Super Romance®

Exciting, emotional, unexpected!

YES! Please send me 2 FREE Harlequin Superromance® novels and my 2 FREE gifts (gifts are worth about $10). After receiving them, if I don't wish to receive any more books, I can return the shipping statement marked "cancel." If I don't cancel, I will receive 6 brand-new novels every month and be billed just $4.69 per book in the U.S. or $5.24 per book in Canada, plus 25¢ shipping and handling per book and applicable taxes, if any*. That's a savings of close to 15% off the cover price! I understand that accepting the 2 free books and gifts places me under no obligation to buy anything. I can always return a shipment and cancel at any time. Even if I never buy another book from Harlequin, the two free books and gifts are mine to keep forever.

135 HDN EEX7 336 HDN EEYK

Name _____ (PLEASE PRINT) _____

Address _____ Apt. # _____

City _____ State/Prov. _____ Zip/Postal Code _____

Signature (if under 18, a parent or guardian must sign)

Mail to the **Harlequin Reader Service:**
IN U.S.A.: P.O. Box 1867, Buffalo, NY 14240-1867
IN CANADA: P.O. Box 609, Fort Erie, Ontario L2A 5X3

Not valid to current subscribers of Harlequin Superromance books.

Want to try two free books from another line?
Call 1-800-873-8635 or visit www.morefreebooks.com.

* Terms and prices subject to change without notice. N.Y. residents add applicable sales tax. Canadian residents will be charged applicable provincial taxes and GST. This offer is limited to one order per household. All orders subject to approval. Credit or debit balances in a customer's account(s) may be offset by any other outstanding balance owed by or to the customer. Please allow 4 to 6 weeks for delivery. Offer available while quantities last.

Your Privacy: Harlequin is committed to protecting your privacy. Our Privacy Policy is available online at www.eHarlequin.com or upon request from the Reader Service. From time to time we make our lists of customers available to reputable third parties who may have a product or service of interest to you. If you would prefer we not share your name and address, please check here. ☐

HSR08

Cole's Red-Hot Pursuit

Cole Westmoreland is a man who gets what he
wants. And he wants independent and sultry
Patrina Forman! She resists him—until a Montana
blizzard traps them together. For three delicious
nights, Cole indulges Patrina with his brand of
seduction. When the sun comes out, Cole and
Patrina are left to wonder—will this be the end of
the passion that storms between them?

Look for

COLE'S RED-HOT
PURSUIT

by USA TODAY bestselling author

BRENDA
JACKSON

Available in June 2008 wherever you buy books.

Always Powerful, Passionate and Provocative.

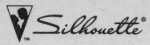

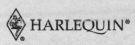

HARLEQUIN Super Romance

COMING NEXT MONTH

#1494 HER REASON TO STAY • Anna Adams
Twins

Coming to Honesty, Virginia, is Daphne Soder's chance to forge a family with her newfound twin. First she must face her sister's protective lawyer, Patrick Gannon. Their confrontations ignite sparks she never expected, giving her a different reason to stay.

#1495 FALLING FOR THE DEPUTY • Amy Frazier

The more Chloe Atherton pushes, the more Deputy Sheriff Mack Whittaker pulls away. However, keen to prove herself, she'll stop at nothing to get a good story for her newspaper—even if it means digging up the traumatic episode in his past. But can she risk hurting this quiet, compassionate man? A man she's beginning to care too much about...

#1496 NOT WITHOUT HER FAMILY • Beth Andrews
Count on a Cop

It's nothing but trouble for Jack Martin, chief of police, when Kelsey Reagan blows into town. Her ex-con brother is the prime suspect in a murder, and Kelsey vows to prove he's innocent. And now Jack's young daughter is falling for Kelsey...just like her dad.

#1497 TO PROTECT THE CHILD • Anna DeStefano
Atlanta Heroes

Waking in the hospital with no memory leaves FBI operative Alexa Vega doubting who she can trust. Except for Dr. Robert Livingston, that is. In his care, she recovers enough to risk going back to finish what she started—saving a child in danger. But if she survives the FBI sting, will Alexa find the strength to truly trust in Robert's love?

#1498 A SOLDIER COMES HOME • Cindi Myers
Single Father

Captain Ray Hughes never expected to return from active duty to an empty house and the role of single father. Thankfully his neighbor Chrissie Evans lends a hand. Soon his feelings toward her are more than neighborly. But can he take a chance with love again?

#1499 ALWAYS A MOTHER • Linda Warren
Everlasting Love

Once upon a time, Claire Rennels made a decision that changed her life forever. She kept the baby, married the man she loved and put her dreams of college on hold. Now her kids are grown and she's pregnant again. Is she ready for another baby? And is love enough to keep her and Dean together after the sacrifices she's made?

HSRCNM0508